THE COLDEST SUMMER

Jenifer Latrice

The Coldest Summer
Copyright © 2020, **Jenifer Latrice**

#JeniferLatrice
#TheColdestSummer

DEDICATION

This book is dedicated to the woman struggling to let go of someone who hurts her soul and breaks her heart. I wrote this book for the woman who is tired of loving someone who no longer deserves her or her energy. Just know that you are beautiful and strong. You are capable of walking away. I hope that one day, you will choose yourself and continue to choose yourself over and over again. Just know that you deserve yourself more than anybody else.

TABLE OF CONTENTS

———————— o ————————

ACKNOWLEDGMENTS

———————— o ————————

I want to take a moment out to acknowledge everyone who has supported me mentally, emotionally, and physically on this journey. I am truly appreciative of every one of you.

You encouraged me to write to find my healing. You prayed for me and cheered me on.

I love you, and I promise I will only play the fool once, and that was it.

The more I wrote, the more I realized that only hurt people hurt other people. If you don't heal what hurts you, you will bleed on people who didn't cut you.

Thank you for your unconditional support.

–Jenifer.

A Word from the Author

———— ✿ ————

Once again, I want to thank everyone for supporting my passion. Truly, writing has always been my passion since I was a little girl. As long as I had a pen and sheets of paper, I was happy. Writing later became my therapy that would help heal many others.

I was able to release my creativity, happiness, anger, and even pain. In addition to my first novel, *Mirror,* this is my second published novel, and there are many more to come.

I want to encourage you to follow your passion and invest in yourself. There's a special gift in you and now is the time to birth it. Now, push!

Facebook: Author Jenifer Latrice
@JTheAuthor

Instagram: @Author_Jenifer_Latrice

PROLOGUE
Just Going to Stand There

♪♪♪

Just going to stand there
And watch me burn
But that's alright because I like the way it hurts
Just going to stand there
And hear me cry
But that's alright because I love the way you lie
I love the way you lie.

♪♪♪

I blanked out and, within that moment, I heard the lyrics to "Love the Way You Lie" by Eminem, featuring Rihanna, playing in the back of my mind.

As I walked closer to the car, with the moon at my back, a red gas can in my left hand, and a lighter tightly enfolded in my right hand, my silhouette on the ground was keeping me company. This was the last straw and the ultimate betrayal. For once, I had no mercy, and every bit of that dissipated, right along with the many tears I'd shed over the years.

"J, please. Don't," a voice echoed behind me. "You got too much to lose. Please, just give me the lighter. You can keep the gasoline.

• • •

Don't throw your whole life away. Please, J, I'm begging you. I feel your pain; I swear I do. If nobody else understands, you know I do," Monica begged. "Unfortunately, it's a cold world and people with good hearts always get hurt the most. I know, Jayla. I know that you didn't deserve any of that! But leave revenge to karma, and know that what goes around always comes back, you just have to let it go, boo. And, trust that, it's going to come back ten times worse. We love you, and this ain't it, boo. I swear this ain't it."

I took a few more steps closer to the car, clenching tighter and tighter to the red gas can.

"You will regret your decision in the morning when you wake up in jail. Think long and hard before you take any more steps closer to that car. Is this really the life you want? Is it really worth it? What will setting that car on fire change?" Monica asked one question after another. "I swear, Jayla, this is just another chapter in your life; don't let it be a life sentence. Time heals all wounds. You just have to find your healing. Your scars will eventually heal; you either allow yourself to suffer or let go of what no longer serves you."

"Tell me how to do it, Monica, because I'm on the verge of saying fuck everything, and honestly, the way I feel right now, I'm willing to risk going to jail and smiling in my mugshot," I said, as tears quickly emerged down my face, angrily thinking about taking my next step toward the car.

"Start by working out again, invest that anger into something constructive, pick up a new hobby, take cooking classes..." Monica said as she fumbled over words and ideas, hoping to convince me.

As I zoned out for a moment, Monica's voice became nothing more than a whispering wind passing by my ears. I was not trying to hear any of that shit. "This muthafucka," I said painfully, peering at the car parked in the driveway.

I closed my eyes and thought about all the people who loved me and all the people who would be without me. As I took in a deep breath, I knew this wasn't me, but the pain from betrayal would bring change to a person, and that's what had taken place. Being hurt repeatedly can create a monster out of anyone, and that's exactly what I am becoming. I am tired of being loyal, tired of the disrespect, tired of the lies, tired of the betrayals, tired of turning the other cheek, I am just tired. There's no pain worse than realizing the person you were once in love with was just there to teach you a lesson.

I opened my eyes and just stared at the car. Monica's voice phased back in. "J, I know how you can heal. Put the gas can down and pick up a pen. Write, Jayla; you love to write. Find your healing in that, not behind bars. Snatch your energy back and put the focus back on yourself. Get caught up on your goals, your dreams, and your grind. You are bigger than this. This is your time to glow up. Tell your story. Free yourself, heal yourself. Remember, there is no better story than a woman who rose from the cold fucking floor she was left on to reclaim her heart and save herself," Monica said, trying to comfort the pain I am experiencing.

I immediately drop the gas can; I know Monica was right. Setting this car on fire wasn't going to change any fucking thing besides changing my home address to an inmate number. I needed to heal, and writing had always been my therapy since I was a little girl. I had a story to tell. I turned around and there was Monica. She was relieved that I had dropped the gas can.

She was walking toward me, with the moon glistening off her. I began to walk in her direction until we met in the middle of the street. She opened her arms and gave me a big comforting hug. "Write your story; don't let this break you down, you must be strong," she whispered into my ear. "You're not the first and you won't be the last to go through this. Write your story with no hesitation in the truth. Help yourself heal, be as open and transparent as you need to be. Expose the raw and real. Don't be ashamed, J. This is your truth. This is the coldest summer…"

As we heard sirens sounding in the distance, we knew then that it was time to go. Monica grabbed me by the hand and we quickly ran back to her car.

"I can't leave my car here," I told her.

"Don't trip, Ashton drove down here with me. Give her your keys because your ass is riding with me. I have to keep my eye on you," Monica said.

"Wait, how did you know I was here?"

"I just had a gut feeling that I would find you here, especially since you weren't answering your phone, and, unfortunately, under the circumstances, Ashton and I got here just in time."

"Wait, how did you find the address?"

Monica laughed and said, "The same way you did," and winked at me.

"Now, let's go write this story. My story is filled with broken pieces, bad decisions, and some ugly truths."

The hardest pill I had to swallow this year was learning that no matter how good to somebody you could be, and no matter how much you loved them, they could turn their back on you, and there's absolutely nothing you could do but suck it up and keep moving forward. Remember this one thing if you don't remember anything else in my story: "There will always be someone who doesn't see your worth, just don't let it be you."

CHAPTER 1
David

D avid stood about six-one, with a golden-brown complexion, board shoulders, and was athletically built. His arms were muscular, his hair had a natural wave he wore in a low fade, and his smile was picture perfect with a dimple on each side, bringing out the enhancement of his facial structure. He spoke articulately and detailed when it came down to speaking and getting his point across. David carried himself with confidence and he always kept it one hundred percent. He took pride in himself on being a real one.

Let me tell you how I met David.

I met David in late 2015. We met in Long Beach, California at the pike around 5:45 pm. I was just up there walking around, enjoying my Saturday off. As usual, just minding my little ole business myself.

"Excuse me, do you know where Mia Tia is?" he asked in this deep masculine voice. As he tapped me on my shoulder, I turned around and said, "I'm sorry, but they closed it down. But if you're looking for another bar, there's one called the Green Box just down the way," I referred.

He was just smiling at me as he listened to me and gave him directions to Green Box. He had the most beautiful teeth that I've ever seen, a picture-perfect smile. His skin was so smooth looking. "Thank you," he said. "Look, I think that you're absolutely beautiful, and I would be crazy not to ask for your number or just for the chance to get to know you. I apologize if I'm being too forward." David spoke on and on asking one question after another before I could even answer them.

I looked him up and down. "So, what's your name?"

"My name is David. What's yours?"

"My name is Jayla, but you can call me J," I responded flirtatiously.

"It's a pleasure meeting you, Jayla." David had this charm about him. I could tell he was a very humble and sincere man.

"Look, do you mind if we take a walk?" David said, looking me.

"I don't know you, and for all I know, you could be a serial killer trying to kidnap me," I joked.

"Kidnap!"

"Yes, I said kidnap, you heard it right."

He laughed. "Look, there's the pier; there are about twenty people over there. So, if I try to kidnap you, everyone will see me. Come on, you don't think I'm that stupid, do you?"

I looked in the direction of the pier and it was literally a few feet away. Plus, looking at David, I didn't mind getting to know him, but I had to play it cool.

"There's a park bench right over there. We can sit on it and talk," David suggested, as we both walked over and sat on the benches. "Tell me about yourself," he said.

I reversed the question quickly. "How about you go first, Mr. David? Tell me about yourself."

He didn't hesitate to elaborate more information about himself. "Well, I guess I could go first. I'm thirty-four years old, with a two-year-old son. I currently work at a manufacturing company. I live in the city of Harbor City. I like swinging, traveling, and football. My favorite NFL team is the Jacksonville Jaguars. I played football back in my day when I was in high school. I was one of the star players. I had scouts looking at me from colleges all over, ready to recruit me. I also used to run track; I was a bad man out there.

"Did I mention that I'm single? I'm not really looking for anything, but I am interested in getting to know someone. I'll be open and honest. I don't have my own place; at the moment, I actually live with my cousin and his wife. About six months ago, my son's mother and I separated, and I moved out. I'm staying at my cousin's house temporarily until I find my own place. So, that's pretty much it about me. Now, it's on you." David smiled.

"Well, I'm thirty years old. I have no children, but someday I would love to have, maybe one or two. I currently work as a nurse. I live in Carson. I played basketball when I was in high school. I love traveling; as a matter of fact, I've been to a few countries and visited about twenty out of the fifty states in the country. I also love learning about business. I was born to be an entrepreneur. I have my own tax business; I worked hard, and invested a lot of money and time to get it up and running.

"Honestly, that's pretty much about me. I just want to be happy, healthy, live a stress-free life, and have money. Oh, and not to mention that I am single as well. That pretty much sums me up."

I looked at David and saw a look of admiration look.

"I had a few businesses myself. How did you market your tax business?"

"It was a lot of trials and errors when it came down to it. I tried business cards, flyers, and Craigslist. But then, one day, it came to me to make signs and put them on lampposts. Once I started putting my signs up, I noticed the change."

David was impressed; I could tell because he was hanging on my every word.

David suddenly admitted that he was impressed. "I've never met a woman so passionate about business as you. I had an electronic business, too. I sold speakers and other equipment. The biggest struggle in my company was marketing the products. So, I'm very impressed because when you spoke about your business, you never mentioned the use of online advertising."

● ● ●

David continues to talk about his success using online advertising.

The more David and I spoke of business, the sparks came. We sat on the bench for hours and hours just talking about business. We were like two magnets in sync with knowledge, quizzing each other on different entities regarding business. I'm sure those who stood around us or walked by would assume we sounded like business partners. Before we knew it, we were still sitting there until the sun went down.

"Look, it's getting late; I truly did enjoy our conversation. I don't want to keep you any longer, and If you don't mind, I'll like to walk you to your car," David offered.

"I enjoyed the conversation, too, David." I stood up. "You're a very smart and knowledgeable man. I can learn a lot from you, and I don't mind you walking me to my car."

"Good, because I truly want to continue talking to you. I have never met a woman who spoke my language in business before and I have yet to meet a man of my age who spoke so passionately and detailed as you when it comes to business."

David walked me over to my blue 2011 Honda Accord.

"I really enjoyed talking with you, Jayla. I was hoping I could have your number so we could continue talking."

I honestly didn't mind; David had my full attention.

He took out his cell phone and handed it to me. "Would you do the honors?" He smiled.

I smiled in return, pressed my number in his phone and handed it back to him. I couldn't help that I was blushing for his smooth and charming tone.

David opened my car door, and I made my way in. "You'll be hearing from me soon," he said, closing the driver's side door.

"I'll look forward to it," I told him.

To be honest, my first impression of David was only based on this single conversation. I thought he was a true gentleman and smart as hell. He really knew his information when it came down to business marketing. I loved it! And, not to mention, he was easy on the eyes.

● ● ●

Not even two minutes after leaving David's presence, my cell phone's notification went off. I grabbed my cell while stopping at a red light. It was a text from David.

"Hi, it's David. Save my number."
Okay, David. I Got you locked in :-)"

Over the next few days, he and I talked day and night. The conversations were exciting and knowledgeable. I felt like a teenager all over again. You know that intense feeling of desire and excitement you sometimes get in your gut? *Man*, I thought, it was nothing like the feeling of fresh puppy love. We would fall asleep talking on the phone, just about random things. David finally asked me out on a real date.

We met up at the Stinking Rose. Since I had never been and always heard great things about it, we agreed to go.

I was to meet David within the next thirty minutes. Once I got there, David greeted me at the door of the restaurant. We walked in together. I swear, it felt like we had known each other for years.

"How was your day?" David asked.

"My day went well. I just took care of some errands and enjoyed my off day as usual. What about you?"

"My day was cool. I went to work, stopped and got a haircut, washed my car, and thought about you."

"Oh really?" I looked up at David. "Why were you thinking about me?"

"You're like a fresh breath of air to me," David said in a calm seductive tone.

I smiled because that was the first time I'd ever heard anyone compare me to fresh air, and I didn't want to tell him, but I had been thinking about him, too. I chuckled.

David surely had a way with his words. Even over the phone, David was very charming, and I found it to be very alluring.

We followed the waiter to our table, and David made sure he walked behind me just to pull out my seat and push me in closer to the table. He was such a gentleman. David insisted that I could order whatever I wanted. And since this was my first time here, I wanted to order everything on the menu. But I wasn't trying to break his pockets, at least, not on the first date, I told myself.

"I'll have some crab legs and a glass of Merlot, please," I told the waiter.

The waiter then turned to David. "Sir, and what will you have?"

"I'll also have crab legs; make that king snow crab, please, and I'll like to have a Coors beer."

The waiter brought bids, a bucket, and a nutcracker for the both of us; it was time to throw down and enjoy our crab legs.

Over dinner, David and I continued to speak about business and more about our lives. We had so much in common; after discovering that we grew up in the same neighborhood and knew a few of the same people, we both found it strange how we never had run across each other before. We sat there for about two hours chatting on a full stomach and enjoying each other's company.

"Wow, thank you for the dinner, David; it was miraculously delicious."

"You're welcome. I'm glad you enjoyed the dinner. I enjoyed it, too. Would you like to go see a movie, if you don't mind? I'm just trying to spend a little more time with you."

"No, I don't mind at all."

I was having such a great time that I didn't want this night to end.

David pulled out his cell phone and Googled movies that were now playing in theaters.

"Have you seen that the movie, *Straight Out of Compton,* is out? Have you seen it yet?" he asked with excitement.

"No, I haven't. Let's go see that."

• • •

Welp, *Straight Out of Compton* it is. We both agreed.
Let's go.

The more and more time we spent together, the more I thought about him on a daily basis, and the more I wanted to be around and with him. His presence was endearing—he was handsome and delightful. He was funny and knowledgeable. He was everything I wanted in a man thus far.

I've always wanted a man I could build an empire with.

As time passed by, David and I spent every day together. We became almost inseparable. Since David's job was closer to my place, and although he was living with his cousin, and spent the majority of his time at my place, I decided to give him a house key. He would always complain about how heavy the traffic was heading home on his commute, so, it would be more convenient for him, and I reveled being with him.

"I have something to tell you J," David said with a straight face, looking into my eyes.

"What do you have to tell me?"

"I love you."

I couldn't believe what David had just told me, and honestly, I felt relieved because my thoughts just slipped right out of my mouth. "I love you, too, David."

We both smiled, looking at each other, and shared a warm steamy passionate kiss. The kissing led to a sensational afternoon of lovemaking, which repeated over and over again throughout the night. I'd never felt in love like this before.

Our bodies were linked like magnets, synced with one another. We shared chemistry, passion, and love, and that alone created ecstasy. Every stroke he poured into my body gave me an all-high feeling. The pleasure I was embracing was undeniable. I could feel the tension of pressure building and my muscles tightening before I finally climaxed.

He turned me on and made sure to please me before he clenched tighter, grabbing a handful of my thighs as he reached his sexual peak.

"Damn, that was good," David said.

We cuddled for the rest of the night.

✱✱✱✱✱✱✱

David nicknamed me Jbaby.

"Jbaby, you're like a fresh breath of air in my life. I've never met a woman to make me feel the way you do."

"Baby, I'm happy that we met, too," I would always say.

"I'm serious, Jbaby, my ex was controlling me; she always accused me of cheating on her. I'll be honest with you; I wasn't the perfect man for her. I did many wrongs in the past. But I also stopped and did everything in my power to gain her trust back, but she didn't believe me. She wanted to control my every move. We constantly argued about any and everything. We were on and off for about six years before we had our son. I get it, I gave her trust issues, but it wasn't right that she was giving me a hard time about seeing my son. She still wanted to be in control. But that's going to soon change. I'll be going to court in a few weeks to get my visitation rights.

"I wish I could have met you sooner…I wouldn't even be going through this."

"I wish I could have met you sooner, too, David. I'm sorry that she is giving you a hard time. Every child needs their father in their life, especially if he wants to be there."

"It's okay, Jayla. I just ask that you never leave my side."

"I won't, David, you have my promise."

A few weeks went by; I noticed a change in David's behavior. He seemed more distant than normal. David's child custody battle had begun, and I could see the heaviness of stress taking a toll on him.

● ● ●

I didn't always know what to do or say because I've never been in a situation like his before. So, I would sit next to David quietly and listen to him release. That was my way of letting him know that I was there for him.

As weeks passed, David became snappier and a lot more distant as he continued with his child support case. I didn't see David every day anymore. His house visits became less. My calls would go unanswered for days. David never gave me any details regarding his child's custody. I just didn't understand, but I just knew that he was under a lot of stress, and as much as I wanted to be there for him, I knew there was nothing more for me to do besides keeping him in my prayers daily and being there if he needed me.

CHAPTER 2
It Started in the DM

"Ricki, I need your help. I found a personal check in David's basketball shorts made out to him from some chick named Raquel Carter," I said. Written in the check's memo was *health insurance*. When I handed the check to David, I looked at him closely in the eye and asked who she was. His only reply was that she was nobody important. He then had the nerve to ask me why I was going through his things. I wasn't actually going through his stuff; I was putting our dirty clothes in the washing machine, and by habit, I would go through all the pockets just to make sure there was no pen or important document left in the pockets. Before Ricki could give me a reasonable answer, I shouted, "I know he is lying, Ricki! And I need to know the truth by any means necessary."

"What do you need me to do?"

"I need you to slide in this Raquel chick's DM on Facebook."

"Did you already find her, Jayla?"

"Yes, I think I did. I want you to tell her that she is beautiful, and be consistent, even if she turns you down. I want you to ask her out on a date. I honestly don't care what you say, I just want to know who the fuck she is and why she wrote David a check out for health insurance."

"You don't play when it comes to your man J, I see," Ricki joked.

"Hell no. I don't! David has been acting really distant lately, and something in my gut is screaming out loud that maybe she has something to do with it. I just need to know. David damn sure hasn't spoken anything more about it; he hasn't been at home, answered my calls, or anything. So, I need to get answers myself."

"All right, I got you, Jayla." Ricki chuckled. "I'm going to see what I can do. Just give me a few days and I'll let you know what's up. I hope nothing serious is going on and that you have nothing to worry about."

"All right, thanks, Ricki. I really appreciate you!"

"I got you, J."

The dial tone sounded as I hung up the phone.

I loved David, but for the last few months, he had been extremely distant. He wasn't coming home every night anymore. And the nights he didn't come home and I'd call him, he didn't even pick up the phone or respond to my text messages. I mean, I knew he was going through his child custody battle with his child's mom and that's extremely stressful. I just needed to know…something just didn't feel right.

✳✳✳✳✳✳

"Okay, let's do this," I said, opening the laptop to search for Raquel Carter's Facebook page. "Raquel Carter! Here you are. You are kind of cute, too."

As I scrolled through Raquel's public profile pictures, I surmised, "Okay, she's cute. I can definitely compliment her smile and eyes."

Raquel was about five-feet-eight inches tall, maybe appearing to weigh around one hundred eighty-five to two hundred thirty pounds, with a brown mocha latte complexion, shoulder-length, naturally curly hair, brown eyes, and shorty was dumb thick.

I didn't waste any time reaching out to Raquel. I started singing out loud, being foolish as usual.

"Aye, it goes, it goes down in the DM (It goes down)
It goes down in the DM (It goes down, it goes down)
It goes down in the DM (It goes down)
It goes down in the DM (It goes down, it goes down)."

"Hi, beautiful. Facebook suggested that we should be friends. And I must admit that when I saw your profile picture, your smile captured my attention immediately. If you don't mind, I would like to add you as a friend. But first, I want to get your permission before I hit the add button. You can't be mad at a man for shooting his shot. You're a beautiful woman and I would like to get to know more about you. Well, that's if you are single, beautiful. Maybe I can take you on a date."

I made sure my words would capture Raquel's attention once she read the Facebook message. Then, I pressed the send button.

I laid it on her pretty thick ass. Now, I just had to wait to see if she would respond.

I truly hoped so for the sake of Jayla that Raquel and David had nothing serious going on. Jayla must have really loved him to go through all this. *She has never asked me to do anything this crazy before*, I thought.

Bingo! Moments later, I received a friend request from Raquel.

Accepted.

You and Raquel Carter are now friends Facebook told me.

"Okay, we are in there now," I said to myself. "Now, let's see if she has any pictures up with David."

I browsed through Raquel's Facebook albums and didn't see any pictures of David, or any man for that matter. Then I looked into her Facebook profile. I felt at ease that maybe Raquel was a part of David's family or even just a friend. According to Raquel's Facebook status, she is single. So, I knew Jayla had nothing to worry about.

I checked my inbox to see if I had any unread messages, and surprisingly, I did.

"Hi, Ricki. Thank you for the compliment. How's your day going? I looked through your pictures and you're pretty handsome yourself. I wouldn't mind getting to know you. And, as far as my relationship status, I'm single. Well, newly single.

"Here's my number: 555-555-5555. You can call me or text me when you're available 😊."

I wasted no time replying back to Raquel's DM. I knew Jayla would be relieved to hear the news.

"Hi, Beautiful. Thanks for giving me the opportunity to get to know more about you. I must admit, I looked through your pictures and you are absolutely beautiful. I'm sorry to hear that you're newly single, but if you'd give me a chance, I'm interested in changing your status, and in the meantime, I'm looking forward to getting to know you. I also do apologize if I'm being too forward, but your beauty was hard to resist. Here's my number as well: 555-555-5512. I'll call you this evening around 6 pm if that's cool."

"Looking forward to speaking to you, Ricki," Raquel quickly responded.

"Likewise, Raquel."

"Ttyl…" Raquel replied with a kissy emoji.

"Damn, this shit is about to go down. Let me call Jayla and tell her that Raquel took the bait."

I logged out of Facebook and dialed Jayla's number.

✳✳✳✳✳✳✳

"Hey, Ricki. What's up?"

"She took the bait," Ricki said excitedly.

"What? That was hella quick."

"Well, you know me; I just laid my charm on her. What woman can resist my charm?" he said proudly.

I laughed. "Ricki, man, you are so silly."

"So, are you ready to find out the truth, J?"

"What did you see while looking through her profile?"

"Well, I didn't see any pictures of him or any other man. We chatted for a second and she told me that she is newly single. She gave me her number and I gave her mine. I told her I would call her tonight around 6 pm. So, this is it, Jayla. We are in there. Are you ready to find out the truth?"

Deep down inside, I was frightened to know the truth. I had a gut feeling that something wasn't right. Although I know that I should always trust my instincts, I wasn't sure if I was ready to confront the truth, especially so soon. I guess it's true when people would say that if you don't want to know the truth, then don't go looking.

"Jayla, I said are you ready?"

I hesitated for a moment. "To be honest, Ricki, I don't know. I mean, damn, I wasn't expecting her to take the bait, especially so soon.

What if there is nothing? Then, I'll feel stupid for not trusting David and he would never forgive me if he ever found out. But also, what if my gut feeling is right and they do have something going on? "What do I do then?"

"Sounds like you're not sure if you're ready to find out, Jayla. What do you want me to do?"

"Just leave it alone, Ricki. I know I was hyped up about knowing the truth, but I think I just need more time to continue watching David's behavior and pattern. Thanks, Ricki, for having my back and being down for me. You are the true MVP."

"Okay, J. If you change your mind, I got you." Ricki looked disappointed; he thought he was doing me a favor. He wanted to talk face-to-face with this Raquel chick and see what was up.

"Thank you, Ricki. I'll call you back later. Okay?"

As much as I wanted to know the truth, I also knew I was head over heels in love with David, and before his child custody battle started, we were good together. David gave me butterflies every time he touched me, looked at me, or even kissed me.

And when we made love; I just loved the way he made my body feel. Maybe I was just tripping or David just needed his space. I couldn't imagine the amount of stress he was going through. Yeah, I'm tripping, I tried to convince myself. As a matter of fact, let me give him a call. It's been a few days since I last tried to reach him.

I picked up my phone. "Siri, call David," I said into my phone. "Calling David..." Siri repeated.

The phone rung four times before the voicemail picked up, stating: *The voicemail belonging to David is full and no more messages can be left.*

Hmm, let me send him a text message, I thought.

"Hey, David. I'm just checking up on you. I haven't heard from you in a few days. I hope you're okay. I Just wanted you to know that

I'm here for you, baby. I love you and I hope to see and talk to you soon."

I waited patiently, hoping David would respond. After a few days, David finally responded to my text message.

"Hi, baby. I know you've been trying to reach me. I've been at my brother's house. I just needed some time to myself to figure some things out. This child custody battle got me stressed out and I just need to get myself together. I hope you can understand. I love you and I'll be home soon."

"Okay, baby. I love you, too! Just know that I'm always here for you," I replied.

I felt a sigh of relief knowing that I have heard from David. I was always excited to see his name appear across my phone, either it was by call or text. Just knowing that David was thinking about me in some way just made me extremely happy. And to think I thought David was out there fooling around, he was just stressed as I thought he was, to begin with. I knew that I no longer had anything to worry about after hearing back from David.

My phone rang four times before I could answer. I looked down at my cell phone. It was Ricki.

"Hey, Ricki, what's up, man?"

"Nothing much, J. What are you doing?"

"I'm just at home, lying across the couch, relaxing."

"I got something to talk to you about."

"Okay, what's going on?" I noticed the quick shift in Ricki's voice, from joking to serious, real quick. "What's up, Ricki? What's going on?"

"Have you talked to your boy lately?"

"Who? David? Yes, he texted me today saying that he is at his brother's house and he will be home soon. See, Ricki, I'm glad my mind said I should leave it alone."

"When was the last time you saw him or heard from him?"

"Maybe a couple of days ago," I said, puzzled. "Why?"

"Well, I know you said you wanted me to forget about talking to Raquel. And honestly, I did. However, she started calling and texting me ever since I hit her up. I responded, and one thing led to another. She invited me over to her house to have a drink last night."

"What?" I sighed in distress. "I thought we agreed to just forget about it, Ricki."

"I know. I'm sorry, but—"

"But what, Ricki?"

"She talked about her recent ex-boyfriend that she still talks to."

"But what does that have to do with anything?"

"J, her ex-boyfriend is David."

"What did you just say, Ricki?"

"I'm sorry, Jayla. But I hope you're ready now to hear the truth about David."

My heart began to beat fast, feeling as if I had a minor panic attack. I wasn't ready. There was nothing in Ricki's voice that screamed this was any good news, only remorse. I took a deep breath and exhaled. "I'm ready, Ricki."

"Well, it turns out that the nights that he wouldn't come home to you, he was going home to her. They were in a serious relationship."

"Wait, how do you know that we are talking about the same person?"

"J, she told me his name and also mentioned that he is going through a child custody battle. I put two and two together, and it's common sense. It ain't no coincidence that two different people have the same name and are going through the same custody battle, Jayla.

• • •

"Besides, I didn't bring any of this up, she brought this up. I think she invited me over just to vent. She had the Jack Daniels bottle and Coke ready. The girl was depressed as if she was going through a mental breakdown, and since she just decided to talk about her ex, I just decided to shut up and listen. And then boom, his name was dropped out of nowhere. I couldn't believe it either, Jayla. I sat there and listened to her through the whole night, talking about his sorry ass. I'm sorry, Jayla, but there's more I have to tell about their relationship.

"His disappearances and not answering your phone calls while he wasn't with you make sense. He was with her. Hmmm, there's no easy way of saying this, Jayla, but she was pregnant by him. She just had a miscarriage about a month ago, and yes, according to her, it was definitely his. She was three months pregnant. Remember the check you found in his basketball shorts? Well, he placed her on his health insurance when he started his new job back in January because she was pregnant. She said he was excited about having another child, especially since his first child's mother is giving him a hard time about seeing his son. To be honest, Jayla, she didn't have a lot of good things to say about him. She called him an opportunist and said he is very argumentative.

"She also complained about him disappearing and not answering when she called him. Looks like that's his pattern. But I have a question for you, Jayla. Did you ever reach out to Raquel?"

"No. Why?"

"Because she said that another woman called her up recently saying that David was her man and that she has seen her number as the last incoming number on his phone. Was that you?"

"No, it wasn't. Every time I would call recently, his phone would go to voicemail and his mailbox would be full."

"I'm sorry, J. I know you really love him. I was also hurt when she told me everything. It took everything in me not to expose his ass to her, but I didn't want to blow my cover.

● ● ●

"So, you are going to dump him, right? Jayla, he is not going to change; so, it would be best if you move on before he continues dragging you along with his bullshit. I'll be damned if I let you get depressed and become miserable like he made Raquel."

I couldn't give Ricki an answer to his question immediately because I was still in shock from the information he just told me about David.

"Jayla, I know you aren't going to take him back after he got another woman pregnant while he was living with you, right?"

I remained silent, unsure of what I should do and where to begin. To satisfy Ricki, I said, "Right. It's over between me and David."

"Okay, good. I'm sorry, Jayla. Just know that he doesn't deserve you. He can't lie his way out of this. Tell his ass 'What's done in the inbox will eventually come into the screenshots and expose his ass." Ricki started to laugh.

And while he laughed, tears began to roll down my cheeks. I was hurt. I didn't know how to feel. I trusted David, loved him. I just needed to gather my thoughts and figure out how to handle the situation. Ricki wasn't making things any better than they were. Instead of trying to understand how I was feeling, his only suggestion was to leave David, and although I was hurting, I knew my heart wouldn't allow me to leave.

"Ricki, I'll call you back later."

"Yes, call me. Let me know what happened once you tell him."

I hung up immediately. I was heartbroken. Although I had a gut feeling something wasn't right, never could I have imagined that this would be "the something" that wasn't right. David told me numerous times that he loved me and that he never wanted to hurt me. He lied to me, cheated on me, and got another woman pregnant. I opened up my heart and my home to him, and this was the thanks I got. "How could you, David? How could you?" I continue echoing, "How could you, David?" hoping I could hear him answer.

• • •

Maybe it was a one-night stand or someone from his past, I thought. I didn't know what to truly think. I remained on the couch, crying my eyes out. *What do I do now? I'm in love with David. How do I just give that love up?*

I sat on the couch for the next thirty minutes, trying to come up with a scenario of how this could have happened. I called the only person I knew who could help me sort out my thoughts and feelings. I called my best friend, Monica. Monica and I have been best friends since kindergarten. It literally was like love at first sight for us. She was the yin to my yang; if one of us got into trouble, then the other would definitely follow. We were in detention together, sick together, you name it, we were always together. She was what I never had: a sister from another mother. We made a pact at the very young age of five that we would show up and show out for each other forever. Twenty-five years later, here we are, still by each other's side.

When it came to relationships, Monica had just about been through it all. By the age of thirty, Monica had been through two failed marriages and had three children. She had been cheated on, beaten, and verbally and emotionally abused by her last husband. Monica experienced relationship blues, time after time again. We'd done countless stakeouts and ride outs together while she was dating Tyrone, who was now her recent ex-husband. I watched her struggle to pick herself back up and strive after their divorce. They were married for five years and had three beautiful children together. Monica would often remind me, "There is no better story than a woman who rose from the cold fucking floor she was left on, to reclaim her heart and save herself."

When it came to love, I was inexperienced. I'd never been as serious with anyone as I had been with David. My only focus back then was getting my education, starting my business, and succeeding. By the age of thirty, I was an established Registered Nurse of seven years, a business owner of a tax business for seven years as well, and a well-known published editor of a local newspaper. I started young and I kept my focus. I had a few boyfriends here and there, but

● ● ●

honestly, I took none of them seriously. I never had a problem of letting their asses go nor did I care if they dumped me. I knew guys came a dime a dozen. Plus, most guys my age weren't looking for love; they were looking for help, and to be blunt about it, just another woman that they could just fuck and use whenever they wanted to.

I knew I deserved more than that. I'd always been so protective with the guys I entertained. I watched my brothers dog women like it was nothing, and I would tell myself, "I'll never let that happen to me" or "If a man cheats on me, I'm leaving." I loved myself way too much to be disrespected. It was funny how you find yourself in life situations that you said you would never be in. People would always say, "Never say never." I now knew how true it was when people said, "You should never say what you wouldn't do or allow something unless you have actually been in such situation, because you never know how you would handle shit until you've experienced it yourself."

I was hurt and distraught. I knew Mo always had a way with words, so I knew she would know exactly what to do or say. She never judged me, and I loved her for that.

I reached for my purse for my cell. "Siri... Dial Mo."

"Dialing Mo..." Siri repeated.

I sat through three ringtones before...

"Hello," Monica answered, with some raspiness in her voice.

"Are you asleep, Mo?"

"Yeah, but what's up?"

"I need you to wake up. I just found out that David is cheating on me and he got another lady pregnant."

"What did you just say?"

"Girl, you heard right."

"I'm sorry, Jayla. *Damn!* I wanted him to be the one for you. You always spoke so highly of him. You two made a cute couple. Damn, sis! I'm sorry."

What did he say when you told him you knew? But, wait, how did you find out?"

"Well, I haven't confronted him yet, apart from me being scared of losing him. I mean, I know he did some fucked up shit and all, but my heart ain't ready to let him go—"

"But J," Monica said, interrupting me. "Didn't you say he got someone else pregnant?"

"Yes, but she had a miscarriage. So, there's no baby now."

"So, what are you going to do?"

"To be honest, Mo, I don't know. She could be lying, but why would she lie to someone she completely doesn't know?"

"How did you find out?"

"Well, about two weeks ago, I found a check in David's basketball shorts from her. At that time, I didn't know who she was or why she wrote him a check. So, I had Ricki slide in her DM and got to know her. And, well, she spilled all the beans."

"Damn, that's slick. Damn, that's fucked up. How do you feel?"

"I mean, I love him. I'm trying to understand why it happened. David and I have not had any arguments, and our sex life is amazing. We were inseparable; I noticed changes with us when the custody battle started, and he started to pull back, putting distance between us. But I thought the distance was there because of the stress he was dealing with and not him dealing with someone else. But now, I know the real reason."

"Have you spoken to him since you found out?"

"I haven't. I texted him a few days ago, and today he finally decided to respond back. And that was earlier; he said he just needed some time to get himself together, that he is at his brother's and I'll see him soon.

"Around forty minutes after receiving that text message, Ricki called me with the news. So, everything is fresh, fresh. I sat down with it for a while, trying to gather my thoughts, but I just can't wrap my head around it, and then decided to call you. I don't know what to do, Mo. I really don't. I've never been in a situation like this before. I've never let a man get this close to my heart and fuck up my feelings and emotions like this. I've always been quick to kick 'em to the curb. But, for the first time, I'm undecided on what to do; maybe David just got caught in the moment. Hell, I don't even know how to tell him that I know. I don't know and I don't want to make excuses for him. But, in all honesty, I'm not ready to walk away from him, either. I love David."

"Look, sis, if you decide to take him back, you won't be the first woman to take a cheating man back nor would you be the last. Just remember, ignoring the red flags because you want to see the good in people will cost you later. Now, here's the catch; if you confront David and tell him that you know and stay with him, he may feel like he can do it again and you'll take him back or he would be genuinely sorry and apologize and tell you it will never happen again. Or, you can just keep it to yourself, try to play cool like you don't know and just watch him. I know that may be the hardest one for you, unfortunately, because you do know. And I know you are heartbroken on the inside. So, instead of trying to figure everything out right now, pack a bag and meet me at my house in one hour. We are going to San Diego to take your mind off things."

"I could definitely use the gateway, Mo."

"Cool. I'll see you soon, sis."

Monica knew exactly the pain I felt. When she found out her first husband, Chad, cheated on her, she was devastated. She gave him everything and did all that he asked her to do to please him. Chad even wanted a threesome; Monica was against it, but she was so deeply in love with him and wanted to make him happy, she did it. Chad wanted it more and more. Monica really didn't care about it after the first time. Although she didn't marry Chad to share him with another woman, with the way it was going, he couldn't just be with one woman. He wanted his cake and eat it, too. I remember one evening Mo called me up crying.

"What's wrong, Mo?"

"Girl, I think Chad is at that bitch's house tonight."

• • •

"Whose house, Mo?"

"I've been finding different women's numbers in Chad's pants pockets. He would always start an argument, tell me how I'm tripping and nagging, and that I needed to stop going through his shit. But fuck, we are married; his shit is my shit."

"Okay, but whose house is he at tonight? And, how do you know?"

"Her name is Keisha. I noticed her calling him, but he wouldn't even answer the phone in my presence. I would ask him who the fuck Keisha is, but he would just lie and say she is his cousin. He is either stupid or thinks I'm stupid. He knows damn well that I know he doesn't have any damn cousin named Keisha. I met his whole family, and there ain't no Keisha."

"But how do you know he is at Keisha's house?"

"I just know. I got a gut feeling."

"Do you have Keisha's address?"

"Hell yeah, I got her address. I got her number and did a reverse look up on that ass. You rolling with me?" Mo asked.

"Let's go."

"Okay, but let me fix my concoction."

"You about to fix a drink?" I asked.

"No, I've been looking at YouTube videos on how to fuck up a car engine. I found a YouTube video where they fixed a concoction and poured it down a car's gas tank, and it fucked up the car. So, I'm about to fix my concoctions with the ingredients they used. And if I see Chad's car at Aja's, his cousin's house, it's going down his gas tank."

"Mo, your ass is crazy. What's in your concoction?"

"I got a gallon of water, a bottle of dishwashing liquid, a pound of sugar, a pound of salt, a can of Coca Cola, and a cup of bleach. I poured everything into the gallon of water and that's supposed to fuck up his engine. He is going to have to remove his gas tank. But by that time, the sugar is going to clog up his fuel injector, and hopefully, the water will mess up the engine, too. I hope his shit doesn't start, and he will either have to call triple-A to tow his car or he will have to call me. And if he does call me, I'm going to introduce myself to Keisha, his cousin. So, be at my house at 10 pm."

I arrived at Mo's house by 10 pm. Mo answered the door, wearing a black dress."

"Ooh. You serious, Mo?"

"Hell yeah, I'm serious. I gave this man everything he asked for and he is still going to cheat? I got something for his ass."

I looked over at the kitchen table and saw the empty dishwashing liquid bottle, the empty boxes of sugar and salt, the bleach bottle, and the empty twenty-ounce Coca Cola bottle. Right in the middle of the table was the one-gallon concoction in a water bottle. Mo had thought this through and now she was ready.

"Mo, look. Have you thought everything through, like what if he catches you pouring this shit down his gas tank?"

"To be honest, then, he will just catch me. And I'll stop and introduce myself to Keisha when she comes outside. Either way, he is going to learn today, or should I say tonight. Who the fuck does he think he is playing with? Let's go, Jayla."

Monica put Keisha's home address in the GPS of her cell phone. Once we got into Monica's two-door black convertible Mustang, we were forty minutes away. Monica continued driving the rest of the way in silence. I looked over and saw tears falling from her cheeks. I couldn't understand her pain, but yet, I felt it. She was hurting and because I loved her so much, I was hurting with her, too. I gently used the back of my index finger to wipe the tears from her face.

"Mo, I got your back, girl. Let's go fuck his shit up."

She looked at me and laughed, and we laughed together. We continued the rest of the journey in silence.

"You have arrived. Your destination is on your left-hand side," the GPS automated lady's voice spoke.

As we pulled up, there was Chad's four-door silver Tahoe.

● ● ●

I looked over at Mo and knew she was hurt. Her face was flooding with tears. It was no denying that her gut feeling wasn't right. I knew how much she loved Chad. And yet, he still found a reason to cheat on her. *I swear, niggas ain't shit*, "I thought. *They have good, loyal women at home and still go sticking their dicks where it don't belong.*

Monica turned the car lights off, but kept the car running.

"Look J, I need you to get in the driver's seat. I'm going to do what I need to do and I'm going to run back to the car. I need you to take off as soon as I make it back to the car."

I could tell Mo was nervous. Hell, we both were. We had never done anything like this before. We both looked around before Monica got out of the car. The street was pretty much dark and there were only a few porch lights on, giving just enough light to see.

Monica took off her seat belt and opened the driver's side door.

She looked over at me and told me to get ready to get in the driver's seat. I unfastened my seat belt and crossed over the center divider as she got out.

Monica ran to Chad's Tahoe and opened his gas tank. I watched her pour the whole gallon of concoction down his gas tank. Monica quickly ran back to the Mustang and I sped out like a bat out of hell into the night.

"Mo, you okay?"

"Yeah, girl, I'm okay. I just can't believe his ass. He had the nerve to tell me that he wasn't coming home tonight because he was spending the night at his mother's house. I guess Keisha is both his momma and cousin," Monica said, joking around. "Everything he tells me nowadays is a lie. I can't take it anymore, Jayla. I can't trust his ass, and I'll be damned if I lay down and go to sleep every night with a muthafucka I can't trust. I let Chad use and abuse me for a whole six years. I stayed because I loved him, hoping that he would change. But, he hasn't. And, see where it's gotten me; to the point that I'm putting shit in his gas tank just to catch him cheating. When I felt that uneasy feeling in my gut, I instantly knew he was.

"A woman should always go with her first mind and trust her instincts. Always. A relationship can be so damn cute in the beginning; then boom, you got an attempted murder case. All because someone wants to play with the other's feelings. I've had enough. One of the worst things you can do is let someone think they can be with you regardless of how they treat you. I made up my mind that I'm filing for divorce from Chad. I'm not happy anymore. And this isn't healthy; I won't allow this to interfere with my character."

Monica meant every word she said that night. She was tired, tired of compromising and competing for Chad's attention. If she wasn't going to be his only one, then fuck it and fuck him. I definitely agreed. Hell, men could be so stupid at times.

✳✳✳✳✳✳✳

I pulled up to Monica's house with my purple Chanel duffle bag in hand. It was one of my favorite to-go bags I would carry for times like this. Monica opened the door, reached out her arms and gave me a hug.

"I'm sorry, Jayla. This weekend we are going to forget about all the drama that has occurred and we're going to have a good time. I think this would be good for both of us. Come on in, I'm just about done packing."

"Where are the kids?" I asked, because it was way too quiet in there and that was not the usual for Mo's house. I was used to seeing the kids run around.

"They are at their dad's house this weekend. Lord knows I needed this break. A mother's job is never done, and besides, I have the kids all the time. I had to put our differences to one side and let him have his time with them. Tyrone needs more time with them anyways. I could tell that the divorce has started to affect them, but enough about that. Let me pour you a shot, J. The tequila is on the kitchen counter. Relax and take the edge off."

I grabbed two shot glasses from the kitchen cabinet and I poured my first shot. I drank it and later poured a second glass for both Monica and me.

Monica came out with her Louis Vuitton suit case in one hand and her keys in the other. "I am ready."

"All right, but first have a shot with me," I demanded.

"I just want to say thank you, Mo. I mean really, girl. You have had my back and I appreciate you."

Monica interrupted me. "Sis, we have always had each other's back since kindergarten; nothing ain't changed. This is nothing new. This is just what we do. So, drink up another shot for the road and let's go."

We both threw our tequila shot back and headed out. Once we jumped into Mo's convertible Mustang, my phone rang—it was David.

"Fuck. What should I do?" I asked Monica, panicking.

"Answer it and play it cool. See what he wants."

"Hello."

"Hey, baby, what are you doing? I'm at the house and you're not here. I was just wondering when you will be home."

"It's good to finally hear your voice," I told him. "I'm actually heading to San Diego right now. I won't be home 'til Monday morning."

"What's out there?"

"I have a few things on my mind and I need to just get away and think."

"Is everything okay?" David asked, with concern.

"Hmm, to be honest, it's not, but I prefer not to talk about it now. I'll be back on Monday and I will tell you all about it. Looking forwarded to seeing you then."

"Okay, baby. Have a safe trip. I guess I'll just see you on Monday. Bye," David said, as he hung up the phone.

"What did he say?" Monica asked.

● ● ●

"Nothing much; just wanted to know where I was and when I was coming home because he was at the house waiting for me."

"He has the nerve to question you? How long has his ass been gone?"

"About a week or so."

"Exactly. He doesn't get to just call and say, 'Come home' when he feels like it. He really has the nerve."

"I need you to focus on Jayla this weekend. This trip is all about you. Deal with everything else when you get back. Use this time to figure out what's best for Jayla. Because, regardless of anyone else's opinions, the decision is yours. I'll support you in whatever you decide to do," Monica said as she turned the music on, putting on our favorite turn up playlist. She dropped the convertible top and we rode off into the sunset onto the 405 Freeway.

Man, this is just what I need.

CHAPTER 3
Mommie, Sorry!

I looked down at the two pink lines in disbelief. "I'm pregnant. I'm going to be a mother. Oooh, shit! Oooh, shit. I'm going to be a mamma," I echoed as I touched my stomach. I wondered how far along I was because I was only five days late. I turned sideways, looking in the mirror, poking out my stomach, trying to get a visual of myself growing throughout the pregnancy. looking in the mirror, I smiled at myself. "I'm going to be some little person's momma," I said, still finding it hard to believe.

Just as happy and excited I was the next moment, my smile soon disappeared and my reality set in. How was I going to tell David I was pregnant? Just weeks prior, he mentioned he wasn't ready for any more kids. I didn't want him to think that I purposely got pregnant. That was never my intention. David already had a four-year-old son. He was a great father, and that's one of the things I loved about him the most. He made sure he fought good and hard during his custody battle for his rights for his son. I'm not sure if he would be as excited as I was to know that we were now expecting.

"Fuck it," I said, as I continued looking in the mirror. My mind was made up—I was keeping our baby. I always dreamed of having a child someday. Now, I just had to tell David the news.

I searched through my black leather Michael Kors purse for my cell phone. There it was, fumbling across my lipstick and iPhone charger. I proceeded to call David's phone.

"Siri, call David," I said into my phone.

"Dialing David," Siri responded.

I took a deep breath, not sure of how I would even start the conversation. This was my first time being pregnant. I always imagined telling my husband face-to-face the exciting news, and we would be so happy together, hugging, kissing, and celebrating, but David wasn't my husband. Hell, at times, I wasn't even sure if he was my boyfriend or not. David was a man I was in love with, who lived with me, and fucked me every day. We exchanged the, "I love you," and even talked about marriage, kids, and growing old together, but from the looks of how things were going, I wasn't sure if that was going to happen. We had our fair share of problems and I knew we weren't always on the same page, and that's what kept us stuck and not moving in the marriage direction.

I held the phone up to my ear, listening to his phone ring until I got his voicemail: "Please, leave a message after the tone, beep."

"Hey, babe. I have something to talk to you about. Give me a call back when you can. I love you." I hung up. I took a deep breath and exhaled. A few short moments later, my phone rang— it was David.

"Hey, baby. How's your day going?" I asked.

"It's going well. I'm just out with the family right now, eating at Lucille's Bar-B-Que. What are you up to? If you are free, come up here."

"I'm not feeling so well, David. When you are done, can you meet me at the house? I really have to talk to you about something."

"Is everything okay?" There was hesitancy in his voice.

"Hmmmmm, yeah, but I will talk to you once you're here."

"Okay, I will be there shortly."

"Okay, baby. See you soon."

● ● ●

I was nervous, happy, excited, anxious, and scared, all at the same time. I didn't know how David was going to respond. He told me stories of other women he dated, and how he would talk them into getting abortions or they would just volunteer for the abortions because they were not ready. He bragged how easy it was to get off and not deal with the responsibility. I didn't believe in abortions, and just in case he tried to talk me into having one, my mind was already made up. I'm keeping our child.

A few hours later, as I was laying in bed, I heard the front door open. It was David. I got out of the bed to meet him in the living room. I greeted him with a hug and kiss.

"Hi, baby. It's good to see you."

"Is everything okay?" He looked worried.

"Have a seat, babe. I have to talk to you about something."

David walked over to the couch and sat down with a puzzled look on his face. I sat next to him and faced him, looking David directly in his eyes.

"David, I'm pregnant…" I paused, waiting for his reaction and response.

David just stared at me. Eventually, he broke his silence. "Are you sure?"

"Yes, I left the pregnancy test in the bathroom for you to see yourself."

"Why didn't you tell me to come home immediately when you found out, Jayla?"

"I was in shock and wasn't sure about how you would respond. So, I just needed some extra time."

David got up from the couch and headed to the bathroom to see the test results. I followed him. He picked up the pink pregnancy test I bought from the Dollar Tree earlier in the day, and there it was: one strong pink line and one faint pink line. I watched David's facial expression, but I was unable to read him. I didn't know what was going through his mind. I knew that no matter what he would say next, I was keeping our baby.

David's mouth opened. "Why are you lying to me about being pregnant, Jayla? You are not pregnant."

"David! I'm not lying to you about being pregnant. My period is five days late. I have no reason to lie to you."

David took a picture of the pregnancy test with his phone and sent a text message to someone. Moments later, he received a response that confirmed what he felt to be true, that I was lying about being pregnant. David dated a lot of women in the past who were in the medical field. I didn't know who he sent the picture to, but they replied to him. That move he made was just plain out disrespectful. Who called their ex for something that had nothing to do with them? I walked out of the bathroom in disbelief.

"David, seriously? Is it really that serious that I would lie to you about being pregnant?"

"I don't know, you tell me, Jayla."

"Look, David. I don't have to lie to you…for what? I took the test earlier in the day, and that's why the second line is faint. I'm only five days late, David. My HCG hormones are not even that high yet."

"You're lying, Jayla. Who sent you to destroy my life?"

"Destroy your life? What? Really? What the fuck, David? Now, I'm trying to destroy your life?"

David walked over to the kitchen with one hand pressed against his forehead and the other on his waist.

"Listen, David. I'm not lying to you. I have no reason to."

"You know I don't want any more kids now, Jayla."

"Look, we both know this wasn't planned, David. You already told me that you weren't ready for any more kids, but you damn sure know you didn't pull out, either, and I wasn't on birth control. David, I'm keeping it."

David dropped his hands to his side and looked straight into my eyes. "So, you have already made the decision to keep it without asking me how I felt?"

"David, I know how you feel already. You don't want any more kids right now, but I don't believe in abortions. I completely understand you're mad and not in any position to take care of more. I just don't believe in abortions or adoptions."

David was very upset and so was I. For the last hour or more, I had to prove that I wasn't lying, even though David wasn't convinced.

"Look, Jayla, I'm not ready for any more kids. You're going to be a single parent raising this child yourself. I can't do anything for it. I can barely take care of my son right now. I don't plan on telling my family about the baby, either." He shook his head. "Fuck, Jayla, I didn't want to be like my father."

"And I never wanted to be a single parent, David."

David still wasn't convinced that I was pregnant. "Jayla, I still think you're lying to me."

"Look, David, we can go and do another pregnancy test right now and I can pee in front you."

"Shit, let's go get one then."

I couldn't wait to prove him wrong. I knew I had nothing to lie about.

✳✳✳✳✳✳✳

The ride to the local Ralphs Grocery Store was very quiet, but the tension was thick. We were both out to prove our truth. I didn't expect this outcome from David. I surely knew he wasn't going to like to hear that we or I was going to have a baby, but I damn sure didn't expect him to tell me I was going to be a single parent or that I was out to destroy his life.

Really, David!

I always heard the saying, "Be careful who you sleep with," but I never expected this from him. But, then again, you really don't know a person until shit happens, and shit was definitely happening tonight.

I looked over at David, and he had a deranged look on his face while driving. I decided to break the silence. "Look, David, I'm not trying to make this situation more complicated than it has to be. I just want you to know that I'm not lying to you. You may have had women from your past lie to you about being pregnant, but I'm not. This is my first time being pregnant."

David looked at me. "Get out the car."

"What?"

"We are here. Let's go get this test done."

We both walked into Ralphs Grocery Store. I walked in ahead of him. Once I entered the store, I headed to the feminine hygiene section, and David followed me. We agreed we would buy two tests in the event something happens to one.

Since it had been a long day and even a longer night, I looked at my phone—11:45 pm. I was just ready to get home, take the test, and go to sleep. I could feel the stress taking a toll on me, and I was tired and didn't want to argue with David anymore.

David and I made it back home.

"Okay, Jayla, let's get this over with."

David took one pregnancy test out of the pink and blue clear pregnancy test box. As much as I was anxious about taking this pregnancy test again, I couldn't pee. I drank about three cups of water, and twenty minutes later, I was ready to prove to David that I wasn't lying. I sat on the toilet, while I held the test stick between my thighs to catch the pee. David stood next to me and stared the whole time. Once I was done peeing, I placed the urine-filled test on the bathroom sink. We had to wait at least three minutes before we could get the results. This was the longest three minutes in my life; it felt more like thirty minutes. Each time we checked—no results. We finally checked the last time and we got our results. I was indeed pregnant.

"See David, I told you!" I yelled.

"I'm sorry, Jayla. I've been lied to so many other times. It was hard for me to believe you."

"I told you, David, I didn't have any reason to lie to you."

As thankful as I was to prove David wrong that I was indeed pregnant, I also knew that he told me I was going to be a single parent. That night, David slept on the couch and I slept in the bedroom. We both needed our space to cool off and think about what was to come next.

✶✶✶✶✶✶

Many days passed and it was very awkward between David and me. David decided it would be best if he gave us some space.

I made my first doctor's appointment; I needed to see how far along I was and to check on the baby's health. I hadn't spoken to David in days since we had taken the test.

✶✶✶✶✶✶
✉

"David, I made my doctor's appointment. It's going to be on this Thursday at 3 pm… If you would like to join me, I could use the support." I sent the message.
✉

Hours and days passed by; still no word from David.

✶✶✶✶✶✶

I looked in the mirror before heading to my first doctor's appointment, I was still couldn't believe I was going to be a mom. I was excited and sad at the same time, but no matter the outcome, I knew I would be a great mother to my child.

"Today, I get to see you for the first time inside of me. I am so excited and a little nervous, too," I said, while rubbing on my belly. "Your grandmother is going to be there, too. I think she is way more excited than I am. Her baby is having a baby. I pray you grow healthy. I promise to always protect you and eliminate any stress. You stay strong and healthy. Mommie loves you *so* much." I was very happy.

****

"Jayla Jones," a nurse called out, with a clipboard in her hand.

"Hi, I'm Jayla."

"Please, follow me, Ms. Jones."

I followed the nurse down the hallway, unsure of what was next.

"Have a seat here. I need to ask you a few questions.

First, I would like to introduce myself. My name is Nurse Smith. I am one of the nurses working with Doctor Sam. Also, I would like to say congratulations on expecting. I'm going to ask you a few questions regarding yourself and the father. Would you like to bring the father in from the waiting room?"

"He couldn't make it. He couldn't take off from work. It's just me and my mom, and she is outside in the waiting area."

"Ooh okay, we can continue without him. First question: when was your last period?"

"My last period was on April 14."

Nurse Smith looked at the calendar and wrote down today's date, May 31, 2017.

"What is your husband's name?"

I corrected Nurse Smith. "He is not my husband, he is my boyfriend, and his name is David Newburyport."

"Ooh, I see," she said. "Next question. Do you drink or smoke?"

"I drink wine sometimes, and no, I don't smoke."

"Well, Ms. Jones, we are done here. I'm going to take you to the exam room to get your height, weight, and blood pressure. And there, Doctor Sam will examine you. Please follow me."

I followed Nurse Smith to the exam room. I was both happy and sad at the same time. I was doing this without David there with me. I was scared; I didn't want to be a single parent, but I also knew having an abortion wasn't on the table for me, either.

"Okay, Ms. Jones, please wait in here. Also, if you can change into the gown, the doctor will be in shortly to examine you."

I lay on the exam table after changing into the gown. I closed my eyes and reminded myself, "You've got this, J."

My mom was a single parent and many single mothers had been here before and made it. With or without David's help, I had to remain focused and strong.

There was a knock at the door.

"Come in," I said, as if I were at home.

"Hi, Ms. Jones. I am Doctor Sam. I will be performing your ultrasound today. Are you excited to see your baby for the first time today?"

"Yes, I am."

"Will the father be joining you in this wonderful experience?"

"Unfortunately, no, he won't. He couldn't get off work today."

"Too bad, but you will definitely leave here with an ultrasound picture to share with him. So, I need you to lay back, scoot all the way to the end of the table, get comfortable, and relax as much as you can. I'm going to perform a Transvaginal ultrasound. I'll be able to see your fetus attached to your uterus. Please, place your feet in these silver stirrups at the end of the table and take a deep breath."

Doctor Sam grabbed his transducer and placed lubrications all over it.

"Okay, Ms. Jones, it may feel cold and a bit uncomfortable, but just relax so I can get some internal images."

Once Dr. Sam placed the transducer inside my uterus, he moved it up and down and side to side. For a brief moment, I experienced something sexual that I had never experienced before. I chuckled and felt slightly embarrassed.

"Okay, Ms. Jones, I found your fetus." Doctor Sam pointed at the video display screen and zoomed in. "This is your uterus, and if you look closely, I'll zoom in more, there is your fetus. Due to its size, you are approximately eight weeks pregnant."

I stared at the ultrasound. There was my baby. I was in love instantly. I used to hear my friends say, "Until you have you a baby, you will never experience what real love feels like," and it wasn't until that moment that I experienced true love. I was in love already.

"Would you like to hear the baby's heartbeat, Ms. Jones?"

"Yes, I would love to."

"Okay, here it is."

The tiny, rhythmic heartbeat from the ultrasound was music to my ears, an outward sign that a new life was growing inside me.

Tears of joy filled my eyes. I was in love and it felt so right for the very first time. Nothing else mattered; I didn't care about anything or anyone as much as I cared about this beautiful creation growing inside of me. I was going to be a mom.

"Are you okay, Ms. Jones?"

"Yes, I'm wonderful."

Doctor Sam handled me some tissue. "I've printed out three sonograms for you. Your expected delivery date is January 14, 2018." He pulled three photos from printer and handed them to me. "Here are your sonograms. I'm going to start you on prenatal care and direct you to go get some lab work done. If you have any questions, please feel free to contact the office and we will assist you. Once again, congratulations. I'm going to step out while you get dressed, but please stop by the receptionist area and pick up your prescription for your prenatal care and to schedule your next appointment."

I stared at the sonograms, happy as ever.

● ● ●

I touched my belly, overwhelmed. "I don't care if you're a boy or a girl. My only concern is that you're going to be happy and healthy. Momma is going to make sure of that."

I walked out of the examination room, picked up my prescription, and made the appointment for my next visit. I met up with my mom in the waiting room. She looked at me, smiling. I could tell she was just as excited as me. I handed my mom the ultrasound pictures and she started to cry, too.

Although she was already a grandmother of ten grandchildren, I was her only daughter and this would be her first grandchild from me.

"Mom, I need to use the restroom before we leave." I took a copy of the sonogram and headed to the restroom. I took out my cell phone and called David. His phone continued to ring until the voicemail answered. "David, I'm at the doctor's office. I texted you about my appointment a few days ago and I haven't heard a response from you. So, I figure I would call you and let you know how everything went. I'm eight weeks pregnant; the due date is January 14, 2018." I hung up the phone, took a picture of the sonogram, and sent it to him, just so he would believe me.

I started to cry again because this was not how things were supposed to be. I understood David wasn't ready for more kids and neither was I, but I'm not running away from the situation. I was just as responsible in creating this child as he was. Fuck it. I reminded myself as I looked in the mirror, "You've got this."

I walked out of the restroom and met my mother back in the waiting area.

"You okay, baby?"

"Yeah, Mom. I'm okay."

A week later, David decided to show up to the house unannounced. I was off that day, laying in bed until I heard the front door open. I immediately got up and there David stood, in his work clothes. He looked at me and I looked at him. It was so much that needed to be said. He bypassed me and headed straight to the bathroom to shower, and I sat on the couch, waiting for him. I knew I didn't want to fight nor argue. I didn't want this conversation to turn awry. Now, there was a baby involved. My goal was to keep my stress level down as much as possible.

I sat on the couch for twenty minutes until David returned from his shower.

"What's up?"

"You tell me, David."

"Honestly, nothing."

I guess since he didn't want to talk about it, I figured I should bring it up. We both knew it was the elephant in the room.

"Look, David, I don't want this to turn into an argument, but we do need to talk. I understand you're not ready to have any more children. I understand your stress about the one you have now, I get it. But we both know this child I'm carrying wasn't planned. I'm not trying to have to keep a man's baby, and you made it very clear that I was going to be a single parent. I think that's fucked up, especially since we both grew up in single-parent homes. I'm not going to force you to be a part of this, if this is not what you want. Hell, I watched most of the women in my life live as single mothers. So, unfortunately, this is the norm. I guess me breaking that fucking cycle wasn't in the plan after all."

"Look, J, you are putting me in a situation that I don't want to be in."

"I am putting you in a situation, David? Really? So, you are trying to say I did this on purpose? Like I told you to fuck me? We both knew I wasn't on birth control and you damn sure didn't pull out. So, what were you expecting to eventually happen? I didn't plan this pregnancy. I am just as responsible as you are.

"Look, if you're going to have animosity watching my belly grow, maybe it's best that we do go our separate ways now. I don't need any extra stress around me, and I don't want to add any extra to your life. Trust me, David, we will be fine without you."

As much as I wanted David to be a part of this new journey with me, I knew it was completely out of my hands. I wasn't going to force or beg him to do anything he didn't want to do. We sat in silence for a moment until I heard him snoring. I looked over and he was knocked out, mouth wide open and all. I looked over at the clock and it was exactly 11:12 pm. I went into the bedroom and grabbed a blanket to put over him and left sleeping on the couch.

I returned to the bedroom and knelt down on one side of the queen-sized bed. I didn't know what else to do. I began to pray.

"Dear God, I ask that You give me strength and direct my path on my new journey into motherhood. I'm scared. I'm scared of going through this alone, raising a child alone, and supporting a child alone. I honestly don't know what's going to happen from here. God, I need You in every step of the way." I took a deep breath and said, "Amen."

For the rest of the night, I lay in bed watching television. The next morning, I woke up and found David laying next to me in bed, just snoring away. I began to climb over David to get out of bed, but he woke up.

"Where are you going?"

"I'm going to watch the TV in the living room."

"Wait, don't go. Let's talk."

I crossed back over to my side of the bed and lay back down, facing David.

"Look, Jayla, I'm not trying to be an asshole toward you. But you know, I have a lot going on with my first child. I mean, I can barely support him. So yes, I am scared, too. I don't want to be an absent father like mine was to me. I'm not ready, Jayla, for any more kids."

"I get it, David. I know you're not ready, either, but I don't believe in abortions. I know you told me about how your other girlfriends had abortions. They are not me, and I'm sorry. I personally wouldn't be able to do it."

"Well, I guess this means we are going to have a baby," David said. The tension was intense in the room.

"We both bite off more than what we could chew. Raw sex is all fun and pleasure until someone gets pregnant."

David remained silent.

"D, I'm about to go to the living room and watch TV". I crawled back over David to get out of bed.

David went back to sleep for a few more hours until it was time for him to go back to work, and I fell asleep in the living room. The pregnancy really made me tired all the time. I didn't want to do anything but sleep. I woke up to see David leaving for work.

"Jayla." David patted me on my , waking me up. "Go lay back in bed. I'm about to go to work."

I looked at the clock and—it was 11:30 am. "Okay, I will."

David walked over and gave me a kiss on the forehead as I lay on the couch.

"Have a good day at work," I whispered.

David walked toward the front door and said, "Thank you. I'll see you tonight."

"Okay, David."

I was too tired to get off the couch and go back to the room. I continued to lay on the couch, telling myself I wouold not move until it was time to pee.

The phone rang.

Who is this calling me? I searched the couch for my phone.

After a few rings, I found my cell phone. It was David calling.

He literally just walked out the door some seconds ago. What's wrong? I thought.

"My truck won't start. Can you take me to work, please?"

I honestly didn't feel like moving, but instead of being honest with him, I said, "Sure, let me put on some clothes and shoes. I'll be out shortly."

● ● ●

David's place of work was about forty-five minutes from the house on a good day, with no traffic. I put on my shoes, grabbed my keys, and headed out. I met David in the back parking structure.

"Here are my keys. You are driving," I told him.

"I need to get a new car, J. My car is so unreliable. This is the second time this week that my car won't start. I really need to get this credit repair business up and running so we can start making some real money, Jbaby. I am tired of barely having enough, and when I finally do get an extra few dollars, something always come up. Let's get to the transporter, J."

David always referred to making money from the business as the "transporter."

David would play Rick Ross' "Transporter" to get us both hyped and motivated to get this money.

Our vision was to use the money from the transporter to fund the investments in stocks and bonds, and buy distress properties down south, fix them up, and rent them out. The ultimate goal was to buy commercial property, one by one, until we bought the block. I believed in David; I saw the twinkle in his eye when he spoke of it. He just lit up like a little kid watching fireworks. This was the David I knew, but I wasn't sure what had happened to him.

"Jbaby, while you're off today, can you look into the credit repair laws and print out any information you find? I want to start doing the necessary research needed to get this business up and running. We are going to get this money," he said excitingly, placing his right hand on my knee. David, looked over at me and smiled. "Jbaby, we are going to be all right."

I smiled, too. "Yes, baby, we are."

I was relieved; the tension was thinning between us, even if it was just in the car for this particular moment. I grabbed my cell and paired it with the car speaker.

"This is dedicated to you, baby. Siri, play 'Transporter,'" I said.

Siri responded, "Playing 'Transporter' by Rick Ross."
David was hyped.

♪♪

"One time for the niggas that's huggin' the block
Two times for the boys that bubblin' rock
Three times for the G's including myself
Four times for the brothers that's reachin the wealth
Five times for the hustle I taught it myself
Transporter I bought it myself
I bought it myself".

♪♪

I watched David rap the whole song. He had so much passion behind it. He put on a concert with just that single song. The forty-five-minute drive felt like twenty minutes and we pulled up to his place of work.

David looked over at me for the last time before getting out of the car. "Can you pick me up tonight around eight?"

"Of course, baby, I've got you."

David leaned over one last time, and kissed me on my forehead and then on my lips before he made his exit.

"Have a great day at work," I said.

"You, too, baby. I'll see you tonight."

I went from the passenger's seat to the driver's seat. I played Rick Ross' "Transporter" one more time as I drove off. I looked through the rear view mirror and David was walking through the door with a smile on his face. It made me happy to see that David was happy. I got it now; he fought internal battles that I sometimes knew nothing about, and, at times, he would lash out at me and I never understood why.

I knew he got frustrated when it came to money and wanting to support his family, and him not being where he wanted to be in life. I knew that his child's mother was making things hard for him as well. He had a lot on his shoulders, too. All I ever wanted to be was his peace.

For the next couple hours, while I waited for David to get off work, I looked up different laws related to credit repair. I listened to a few short audio books regarding credit repairs for dummies. I wanted to be knowledgeable and resourceful to David. I cooked David's favorite meal: steak and potatoes with a salad, I put a cold beer in the refrigerator, cleaned up the house, and washed our clothes.

I was exhausted and needed at least an hour nap before it was time to pick up David.

Being pregnant has made me more tired than ever. I was only eight weeks along. I had twenty-eight more weeks to go. I fell asleep in the living room on the couch.

The phone rang and I woke up in a panic. "Shit, what time is it?" I looked at my cell phone and it was David calling.

"Hey, baby. Where are you? I am off work."

"Damn, I overslept. I'm getting up right now. I'll be on my way."

"Okay, baby," he said, before I hung up the phone.

Shit, it felt like I just closed my eyes.

I grabbed my keys, slipped into my house shoes, and rushed out the door.

David got off work about thirty minutes ago.

I finally arrived to David's work. He was standing out in front with his cell phone in his hand. Once he noticed me, he put his cell phone into his front pocket and started walking toward the car. I got out of the car, gave David a kiss on the cheek, and moved to the passenger seat. I moved through the driver's side door, made my exit, and sat in the passengers' seat. David never liked me driving whenever he was in the car, so I always let him drive when we were in the car together.

"How was your day?" I asked him.

● ● ●

"It was okay. I'm tired."

"Trust me, I do understand that feeling."

"I just want to get home, relax, and get a good night's rest."

"I cooked your favorite meal, baby: steak and potatoes with a side salad. I even put a cold beer in the refrigerator for you."

"Thank you, baby."

I could tell David was exhausted and really didn't have a lot to say. We rode home in silence.

Once we got home, David kicked off his shoes and socks, took off his pants and boxers, removed his work shirt and wife beater, and headed straight to the shower. He left a trail of dirty clothes that led straight to the bathroom. While David was in the shower, I warmed up his dinner, turned on NFL Network on the Xbox so he could watch the football game he missed. Last, but not the least, I grabbed his beer out of the refrigerator.

I set the TV tray up and placed his hot food on the table alongside his beer. Right in front of the television, David had everything he needed to enjoy the rest of his evening.

"Baby, the food smells so good!" he yelled from the bathroom. "I can't wait to eat; I'm starving." David came out of the bathroom with a towel wrapped around his waist. He sat down on the couch, pressed play on the remote control, opened up his beer, and dug right into his loaded potato and steak.

I sat next to David, still tired as hell. I closed my eyes and was knocked the hell out for the rest of the evening. It was already around 11:00 p.m.

"J, wake up. Let's go lay down." David shook my shoulder. "Get up.

"What time is it?"

"It's 3:00 a.m."

I got off the couch, still half sleep. David guided the way as he turned off the lights and television. I followed him in complete darkness. We finally reached the room; I got in bed first and he then

• • •

followed. I faced toward the window and my back was against David. I felt a poke, and I know what that meant; David wanted some dessert.

✳✳✳✳✳✳✳

Morning came and I heard David on the phone.

"My car won't start; I need to tow it to the shop. I'll be there to pick up Kevin around 1:00 p.m."

He walked back into the bedroom. "J, we are going to get my car towed to the shop, but I also have to pick up my son today by 1:00 p.m. I'm not sure if my car will be ready or not. If it's not, I'm going to need you to take me to pick him up."

"Okay," I replied.

"Start getting dressed; I've already called triple-A, and they said they will be here in forty-five minutes to an hour."

"Alexa, what time is it?" I yelled out.

"The time is 10:23 a.m."

An hour later, the tow truck came and took David's car to the shop.

David then learned that his car needed a major tune up and it wouldn't be ready for pickup until Monday.

That Saturday, I was off from the hospital. I spent time with David and his son. We went to eat, to the beach, the movies, and Toy 'R Us to get Kevin some new toys. It was just the three us, I mean… four of us, including the child I was carrying. It was going to be our new family member. I just loved how David loved his son. He was very attentive; he's the type of father I wished I had growing up. I loved Kevin, too. I grew attached to him, and he's such a joy to be around, a cute and smart kid.

I wondered how our child would look. If it were a boy, I hope it had David's body structure and his charming smile. If it were a girl, I wanted her to look like me; yet, still like her dad. As the day came to

● ● ●
49

end, I dropped David and Kevin off at his cousin's house. David's car was still in the shop until Monday, and I was on duty at work on Sunday.

"Get home safe," David said, as he exited the car. "Let me know when you made it home."

"I will."

Kevin waved and said, "Bye, J."

"See you later, Kevin."

On my way home, I felt relieved that even though our situation wasn't perfect, we were working it out.

It took me no time to get home.

"Hey babe, I made it," I sent as a text a message.

"Great," David replied immediately.

"I'm tired. I'm about to shower and go to sleep."

"All right," David responded.

The next morning, I got up and got ready for work. Though I was tired as hell, I still managed to get out of bed in time and make it to work on time. That day, I worked on med surg. My work assignment was heavy because we were understaffed. As the morning went on, I started feeling cramps in my lower stomach. This was the type of cramps I would feel before my period started. I knew my period wasn't coming because I was pregnant. I went to the restroom to check just to make sure, and I was spotting.

"What the fuck?" I said to myself. "This can't be my period coming on. I'm pregnant!"

I came out of the restroom and asked my colleague, Nicole, if she had ever experienced bleeding while she was pregnant. She told me that she had before, but it was just implantation bleeding and it was nothing to worry about.

• • •

I was worried; I knew I was under a lot of stress, and I didn't want it to interfere with the health of my child.

I texted David.

✱✱✱✱✱✱✱

11:05 am: David, I went to the restroom and I noticed I started spotting.

11:30 am: I Went back to the restroom, and now, I'm Bleeding.

12:00 pm: You picked up the wrong toy for Kevin.

12:01 pm: The receipt is in the bag, just return it. I'm bleeding; I think I may have to leave work early to the emergency room.

12:30 pm: I looked in the bag, I didn't see the receipt.

12:31 pm: I Just went downstairs and spoke to the doctor. He told me that it's normal to bleed, but if I continue, I need to leave work and get checked.

1:00 pm: Ok.

1:01 pm: All you have to say is just okay? I told you I'm bleeding, and I'm scared.

1:10 pm: Look, J. I have to take care of my son. I'll hit you back!

David didn't seem to care that I was bleeding. Hell, he didn't even want the baby.

I called Monica. She was more of my support system than he was.

"Hey, J. What's up?" Monica answered the call.

"Mo, I'm at work and I started bleeding. I went downstairs and spoke to our Emergency Department Doctor. He told me it's normal in the first trimester, but if I continue, I should leave work and get checked out."

"Have you told David?"

"Yes, but all he was concerned about was me getting his son the wrong toy."

"This fool doesn't give a fuck about you, Jayla. Can't you see that? I swear, if I ever see him, I'm definitely going to cuss his ass out! You don't deserve to be treated like this. My mom once told me, 'I can tell you over and over to leave the situation, but you won't. One day you will wake up and realize that this isn't what you want to feel like anymore and you'll be done.' I think it's important you hear this, Jayla."

"I know, Mo. I know."

"Look, if you leave work early, let me know, and I'll meet you at whatever hospital you go to. You shouldn't have to go through this alone."

"Thank you, Mo."

After Mo and I got off the phone, I went back to the restroom. I started to bleed a lot more and started feeling cramps in my lower abdomen. I looked in the restroom mirror while rubbing my belly. "What's going on, Champ? You got me worried."

I walked out of the restroom and talked to my charge nurse.

"Sarah, I haven't shared this with you, but I'm pregnant. I started bleeding this morning and it continues to get worst. I'm going to have to leave work."

"Jayla, you can leave now. Go take care yourself. Make yourself a priority. I'll take your patients. Just give me a report and go rest."

I immediately went to Our Sister Hospital, which was twenty minutes away. I didn't want my co-workers to know.

I was hoping my wait wouldn't be long, especially since I have scrubs on. Maybe that would make them show me some compassion. My wait time wasn't long.

"Ms. Jones," a nurse called out as I sat in the waiting room.

"Hi. I'm Ms. Jones."

I followed the nurse as she led me to a room to be seen by the doctor.

• • •

"What brings you in?"

"I'm nine weeks pregnant, and today while at work, I started spotting; then, it started to get heavier."

"Okay, let me take your vitals and the doctor will be in shortly."

"Thank you."

As the nurse was taking my vitals, the doctor came in. The nurse handed the doctor my chart and he read it in silence.

"Hi, Ms. Jones. I'm Doctor Zeek. I just need to ask you a few questions. Are you currently having cramps?"

"Slight cramping, but the cramps are very intense," I answered.

"How long have you been bleeding?"

"It just started today while I was at work."

"I'm going to order an ultrasound, and once I get the results, I'll be back to speak with you more. Do you have questions for me?"

"No."

A few moments after, the Ultrasound technician (specialist) came in.

"Hi, Ms. Jones. I'm Bobby. I'll be performing an ultrasound on you today."

Bobby was an older Caucasian man. He had a white lab jacket and a Mickey Mouse tie.

"I like your tie, Bobby. It's very unique."

"Thank you. My wife bought me this tie twenty-five years ago as an anniversary gift."

"Wow! How long have you two been married?"

"We've been married for about forty years."

"That's amazing. What's the secret to a lasting marriage?"

"Well, what works for us is that she is always right," he said, laughing. "But, in honesty, we communicate and work together as a team every day. I respect her and she respects me. We found out what makes us work because everyone is different. But let me say first, there has to be love, trust, communication, and respect there. That's the key."

● ● ●

"Thank you for sharing."

"So now, let's get to this ultrasound."

As Bobby performed the ultrasound, I was worried about my baby.

I was under so much stress and it had been taking a toll on me lately.

Bobby continued to take screenshots of the ultrasound.

"Bobby, can I ask you another question?"

"Sure, you can."

"Is my baby all right."

"I wish I could give you an answer. I'll get these ultrasounds over to the doctor and he will explain everything to you. But I can tell you this... You're going to be a great mother," he said, winking at me with a smile. "Take care of yourself."

"I will. Thanks, Bobby."

I sat in the examination room until the doctor got the results.

"Ms. Jones, I got the results back, and the fetus still has a heartbeat. I'm going to put you on bed rest for a few days. You are currently experiencing a threatening miscarriage. If you continue to bleed heavier and things get worse, please, come back in immediately."

"Thank you, Doctor."

"Do you have someone to drive you home?"

"No, I'll drive myself."

"Take it easy and get some rest."

"I will."

As I stood in front of the mirror in the examination room, rubbing my belly, I said, looking at my belly, "Today, you scared me, my love. I started bleeding while at work; I left work early and went straight to the emergency room to check on you. You're are a strong little soldier already. Hang in there, Champ. Momma wants to meet you in January."

As I was driving home, my text notifications went off and I saw that David texted me.

David: "How are you?"

Me: "I'm okay. The doctor put me on bed rest."

David never responded back.

Once home, I showered and got in bed. I watched television for a while and I looked at the time, it was 9:30 p.m. My cramps became more and more intense. I started to even feel them in my back. I hated that I had to go through this alone.

"David, I wish you were here to rub my back. These cramps hurt," I sent via text.

Two hours later, David responded back. "Why should I rub your back? We don't have a connection like that."

"You're right David, we don't."

I knew David would be expecting me to go on and on, but I wasn't about to waste any more energy going back and forth.

****

The next morning, the cramps still continued. My bleeding got so heavy that I needed to wear a pad. I was afraid. I called David's cell phone, but he didn't answer. I tried it again and again, still no answer. I continued to rest in bed.

At 4:20 p.m., David sent me a text message. "Why haven't I heard from you today?"

"David, I called you twice, and I didn't get any answer. I texted you, but you didn't respond."

"You could have left a message."

"David, I'm still cramping and it's getting worse. I've been asleep most of the day."

"That's not an excuse, Jayla. See, that's one of the problems we have now. You don't know how to communicate with me. If you did, I wouldn't even be such an asshole to you."

"But David, I do communicate with you; you just ignore me."

"No, Jayla, you don't listen to me, and that's the problem."

"David, I'm doing the best I can."

"You can try a little harder. Hell, you don't even make an attempt to please me in bed anymore."

"David, I asked you about what we could do to spice things up, and you just brushed me off."

"You don't even suck my dick right, and sometimes, you're stiff. It's a turn off, Jayla, that you can't please your man right. Look, J, if we are going to make this work, you're going to have to listen to me. I need you to pick me up from my cousin's house by 6:30 p.m.; I should have dropped off my son by then."

"David, the doctor put me on best rest. I can't drive anywhere. I was given orders to take it easy and rest. You can take an Uber here."

"I don't have Uber money. It's going to cost too much and it's a waste of time when you sit at home doing nothing."

"David, I'm cramping and bleeding. I can't."

"See, there you go again not listening to me. Either you pick me up by 6:30 p.m. or we are over."

"I'm bleeding, David, I can't."

"Put a towel on the seat, but you better be here or we are over."

I looked at the time and it was 4:45 p.m. I didn't want to be a single parent. *How can a man say he loves you and be so cold?* I was torn between

• • •

bed rest or picking up David from his cousin's house. I watched the clock and endured the cramps a little bit longer, continuously feeling the pain. I closed my eyes and cried until I couldn't cry anymore. Time moved faster and faster. It was 6:00 p.m. already.

Maybe we can work it out, I convinced myself. *Our child needs his father in his life.*

I got up, put on some clothes, and made my way to David. I couldn't even lie; I was in pain. I questioned his love for me. Hell, I even questioned the love I had for myself. How did I allow this man to manipulate me? I couldn't even give myself an honest answer.

If David and I were going to be a family, I needed to try to make things work.

I arrived at David's cousin's house. I honked my horn and David came running out.

As usual, I went from the driver's to the passenger's seat and reclined the seat.

David and I rode home in silence.

It wasn't until we got home that we had a single conversation.

"J, I'm not trying to be an asshole. But you know we are not ready to have any kids right now."

"We are not, but I don't believe in abortions. We both knew what we were doing."

"J, I'm not ready. I'm having a hard time taking care of the son I already have," he constantly reminded me. "We just need more time. I don't want to be an absent father. I don't want to be like my father."

"And I don't want to be a single mother either, David. We can't change anything, I'm pregnant. We both made that bed and we have to lie in it."

David sat on the couch in silence.

We sat apart as silence filled the distance between us.

"If we are going to raise this child together, you have to listen, Jayla," David said, at ease. "I don't want to be an asshole to you."

"And I don't want you to be, David," I quickly replied.

● ● ●

David leaned over and kissed me on my cheek, then my neck, and slowly started to remove my clothes. He grabbed my hand and placed it in front of his crouch. He was hard and I knew he wanted sex. I was bleeding and cramping, and all he could think about was sex.

"Show me how much you love me, J. Take this dick all in, make it feel wanted by you. Go ahead, put it in your mouth, and make love to it with your tongue," David whispered in my ears.

I went from sucking to us fucking in the bedroom. David wanted to be in complete control.

✳✳✳✳✳✳✳

Afterward, I turned my back toward David. Tears filled my eyes.

He didn't care I was bleeding; all he wanted was that nut. But I was just as guilty because I agreed. I prayed silently that night before I went to bed.

"Lord, I need you. Please, save my baby. Please."

I stayed up most of the night, silently crying. David slept well. He snored the night away.

I woke up around 4:30 a.m., with an urgent sensation of needing to use the bathroom.

I pulled down my panties right before I sat on the toilet. I checked my pad and I was having a full period. I was nervous. This was my first time ever being pregnant. I felt the urge to push like I was having a bowel movement. Unable to hold it, I pushed, then proceeded to wipe myself. I looked down into the toilet and I saw a big blood clot about the size of a mango.

"My baby, my baby, my baby, my baby!" I screamed, while tears ran down my face.

I knew I had a miscarriage.

I didn't want to flush the toilet. My baby was in there. I was ten weeks pregnant, and it ended that day. A part of me was now gone, my whole vibe shifted. I knew things would never be the same for me again.

I knew I should have told David, "Fuck you," when he threatened to end our relationship if I didn't pick him up from his cousin's house by 7:00 p.m. yesterday, even after I told him I was bleeding. I should have seen right through his sinister tactics of him having rough sex with me. This was what David wanted; he wanted me to miscarry, and I fell for his trap.

I stayed in the bathroom for fifteen minutes, staring at my baby in the toilet, and blaming myself for not protecting it from all harm and danger, including from its father.

"I'm sorry, baby. I'm sorry." I grabbed some tissue and wiped myself. Then, I took a shower. I was devastated. What the hell was I thinking?

I knew at that point that it was over for us. The relationship had to come to an end.

He didn't give a fuck about me and that was very clear.

I didn't even give a fuck about myself, and that was obvious. A woman who loves herself would have told the muthafucka to get the fuck on, and raised her baby on her own.

I got out of the shower and looked at my baby in the toilet one last time before I flushed it. It was the most heart breaking moment I've ever had to endure in my life. As the water filled the toilet and flushed everything down, a part of me died.

I came out of the bathroom and lay on the couch. David's alarm clock was about to go off by 5:30 a.m. He had to be at work by 7:00 a.m. Balled up like a baby in fetus position, I was cramping, crying, devastated, heartbroken, I was hurt. I felt like David just robbed me of motherhood, even though I was a willing participant. I lay there until David's alarm went off.

I heard David walk into the bathroom. Moments later, I heard the shower running.

I didn't want to tell David that I had a miscarriage. He wouldn't even care. He wouldn't feel my pain. I didn't even want to give him the satisfaction of knowing that his tactic worked. I just continued to lay on the couch and faced the window, so when David walked into the living room, he couldn't see me crying.

"Why are you lying on the couch?"

"I had to use the bathroom and I didn't want to wake you. So, I just came out 'til it was time for you to get up," I said, with my back to David.

I could hear David walked closer to me as he spoke.

"Why are you lying in that position? What's wrong?"

"I don't feel good. Look, just take my car to work. I don't think I'll be able to drop you off this morning."

David walked over to me and touched my shoulder. "What's wrong, J. Something doesn't seem right."

I turned toward David.

"Why are you crying?"

"I went to use the bathroom this morning and I passed a big blood clot. I think I had a miscarriage."

"Why didn't you tell me?"

"Because, honestly, I knew you wouldn't care."

"I'm about to call in to work right now. Let's get you to the hospital."

David called his job and told them he couldn't make it in due to a family emergency. David went in the room and got me sweats and a T-shirt. He even helped me get dressed. He brought me my favorite slippers and put them on. David got himself ready next.

Between the cramps, the pain, andthe tears, I was numb. I didn't care about going to the doctor, I just wanted to lay there. I deserved to feel what felt like death to me.

"I'm ready. Let's go." David came out of the bedroom into the living room. He helped me get off the couch. "I got you, J. I'm here."

● ● ●

David helped me to the car, and once in, he even helped me put on my seat belt. I reclined the seat all the way back. The cramps were severe.

"What hospital should we go to?" He asked.

"We are going to Kaiser Harbor City."

I closed my eyes during the whole ride to Kaiser.

Every five minutes, David kept asking me if I was okay. Each time, I would tell him no.

I thought, *How am I ever going to be okay from this moment on?* God blessed me with a child and I neglected to take care of it. Resentment and regrets were going to linger around for a while. What if this child could have been the one to cure cancer, or be the next Black president, or was going to change the world? What if... What if this was my only chance to have a kid?

What if...

What if I had just sat my ass at home and said, "Fuck it and fuck you, David?" Maybe I would still be pregnant now, figuring out my journey as a single mother.

****

We arrived at the hospital. David got out of the car first. He asked the EMT standing outside if he could bring a wheelchair to the car. Moments later, David was opening my door, aiding me out from the front seat into the wheelchair. The cramps were unbearable, but I deserved this pain. Once I was in the wheelchair, David rolled me into the hospital and we headed to the registration counter. I pulled out my insurance card and told them the reason I was there.

The young woman who sat behind the registration table handed me a clipboard and pen. "Please, fill out these documents," she said. "I'll make sure you get in right away."

Five minutes later, my name was called. I had not even completed filling out the paperwork. The nurse took my vitals and my temperature. While we waited in the examination room, I lay on the gurney.

We sat in silence. I didn't have anything to say to David, who was looking at his phone. I turned my back to him. I couldn't stand looking at him; I didn't want him to see me crying. I was the only one remorseful. It was my baby I lost.

"Hi, I'm Bobby. The doctor ordered a pelvic ultrasound, and if that's okay with you, I'd like to get started." The ultrasound technician looked at me and remembered me from my last visit. Then, he looked over at David. The last time I came alone, he told me, "Take it easy, I don't want to see you back here again under these conditions." And well, here I was again.

He saw the grief on my face, the exact same look from the first ultrasound.

"So, let's get started. Would you like him to stay or step out?" Bobby asked me in front of David. Before I could answer, David said he would step out.

It was just me and Bobby in the room, as the female nurse walked in as David walked out. It was just the three us, and Bobby was searching for the fetus in my uterus.

"Are you cramping?" he asked.

"Yes, I am."

He shook his head and captured a picture on his monitor.

"Do you see my baby?" I asked.

He looked over at me, and I tried to read him. He gave me a straight face and said, "The doctor will talk with you," and, just like that, he was done with the ultrasound. He looked at me for the last time as he left the room. "Hey, Ms. Jones."

"Yes."

"I promise, you're going to be okay," he said with much compassion.

As the technician walked out, David walked back in.

"Let's talk, David. s there anyone else you were dealing with besides me this year or last year?"

David looked at me, unsure where that question came from. He opened up his mouth and I was ready for the lies.

"Yes," he said. "I was cheating with Raquel."

"The night I followed you from work, where were you really going?"

"I went to go meet some chick off POF in the City of Industry."

I wanted to dig in deeper into the questions and get more detailed answers like him actually confessing getting Raquel pregnant. But I settled for that due to my current circumstance.

"Now, let me ask you the same question," David said.

"Yes, this was yours. I've never stepped out on you. I've always only had eyes just for you and only you. Always from day one."

All David could say was, "Okay."

The doctor walked in moments later with the ultrasound results.

"I'm sorry, Ms. Jones, but you actually had a miscarriage. There is still some of the fetus left in you. I'm sure today, you will pass the rest. I'm going to write you a prescription for pain pills to help with it. Once again, I am sorry for your loss. Do you have any question for me?"

"No. Thank you, Doctor."

He handed me my prescription and told me I was discharged.

I looked over at David just to catch him staring at me. I didn't want to wipe the tears this time. I wanted him to see my pain, the grief.

"Is there anything I can help you with?" He asked.

"No, I'm fine."

"Well, just let me help you get off the gurney and change back into your clothes."

David helped me from the gurney to getting dressed and to the car.

Once in the car, David grabbed my left hand and looked at me. "Jayla, I want more kids; just not right now. I need at least three more years. We can have them, I promise. Once we get married, J. I love you."

I didn't even bother to look his way.

"Look at me, J. I'm going to marry you one day. We will have kids."

I was in pain and nothing even mattered anymore.

On the way home, we made a quick stop to Walgreens to put in my prescription. Once we got home, I went straight to the bedroom to lay down. David went to the living room to watch televisioin.

I lay in bed crying and blaming myself. "I should have put my baby first! That was my priority. I was my baby's protector and I failed. I miss you already. Momma is sorry," I said, rubbing my stomach. "I'm sorry."

You really don't know pain until you've begged God to heal your heart.

For the next few months, it appeared that things had gotten better between us. It felt as if we were finally on the same page. David came home after work every day, we buckled down, and made a business plan for his credit repair business. We had gotten past the hard part; I was so happy, although I lost something so dear and precious to me. Finally, we were heading in the right direction.

Every now and then, David would accuse me of cheating on him. But I've never cheated on him, period. Since the day I met David, he always had my attention. If it wasn't one thing, it was always something else. I honestly thought David would change for the better.

● ● ●

CHAPTER 4
This Muthafucka

"Look, Jayla, I'll get straight to the point. I need to get my duffle bag from your house. I am going out of town in two days and I need it. And, by the way, I got rid of your house key."

"What do you mean by you got rid of my house key, David? Why would you do that?"

"Listen, J, I'm getting married. I can never see you again."

"What do you mean by you are getting married, David? You were just here with me."

"Jayla, no man ain't going to want a woman he can't trust."

"What are you taking about, David?"

"I haven't forgotten about you following me from work."

"David, that was year one of our relationship when I knew you were fucking around on me."

"Let's getting something clear, Jayla. We were never in a relationship; you were never my woman. Why do you think I kept fucking around on you? I made it very clear that I don't give a fuck about you. You deserved everything I did to you. You never had my back or had any good intentions for me. You are just like every other woman I've dealt with. I need to get my shit from your house. So, let me know, or better yet, you can sit that shit outside and I can pick it up off the curb. I don't want to ever see you again. You had your chance, Jayla, and you couldn't be the woman I needed you to be. I needed a woman, Jayla, and that wasn't you."

It felt as if David had taken a butcher's knife and stabbed me in the heart.

Before I hung up the phone on David in rage, I made up my mind that this muthafucka was done disrespecting me for the last fucking time. Tears ran down my face and could feel my heart racing. I was angry, hurt, and confused. I was so sick that my stomach was balling in knots. That muthafucka needed to reap what he had sown.

I housed David, cooked, clean, and fucked him. I was there when he needed me to be there, and here he was going to marry the next bitch. "*Uggghhhhh!*" I screamed.

I picked up the phone and called Monica. It was 1:00 a.m.

"Hello," a raspy voice answered the phone.

"Mo, he is getting married."

"Who is getting married, J?"

"David!"

"What?" she exclaimed, just as shocked as me.

"He had the nerve to tell me that I never had his back, we were never in a relationship, and how he didn't give a fuck about me. He used me, Monica, this whole time. He used me, and now, he is marrying Danielle. I was so good to him, and this is how it ends? I've got something for him. He thinks he can just play with my feelings; he got another thing coming."

"Jayla, don't go get yourself in trouble. Please, don't go to jail tonight."

"Fuck him," I said, as the tears continued to flow. "Fuck him. I got something for his ass that he won't even see coming."

"J, please, don't. I know you're hurt, I know, but he ain't worth it."

"*Nooo*, Monica, this is personal, really personal. I gotta go."

"Jayla!" Monica shouted, before I hung up the phone.

• • •

Monica called back several times, but I let her calls go straight to voicemail. There was nothing she could say to take the pain away. I was hurt and felt betrayed for the very last time. I had had enough of David's shit. He was always so arrogant as if he were untouchable. He walked around as if his actions had no consequences.

I laughed grimly. "This muthafucka."

I grabbed my keys and walked out of the house.

✱✱✱✱✱✱✱

"Shit, I hope Jayla doesn't go to jail tonight. I need to stop her. Let me call Ashton to ride with me."

"Hey, Monica," he answered on the first ring. Caller ID showed him I was calling.

"Ashton, we have to go stop Jayla," I said, panicking. "David told her he is getting married, and she didn't take the news well. Ash, I have a feeling she is on her way to their house to fuck up some shit. We have to stop her."

"What the hell?" Ashton exclaimed.

"I know; I'll explain the rest in the car. I'm about to pick you up. So, throw on some clothes and say a prayer because this can get completely out of hand. I'm walking out of the door now; I'll be on my way."

"Do you know where the bride-to-be lives?" Ashton asked.

"Yes, I Googled her name and found her address."

✱✱✱✱✱✱✱

I pulled up to the nearest gas station, dressed in all black.

"Hi. Can I help you, miss?" the gas station attendant asked.

"Do you sell gas containers here?"

"Yes, we do."

"I'll take the largest one. How much do I need to fill it up?"

● ● ●

"About $15."

"Well, I'll take fifteen on Pump 6. I will also take that lighter."

"Which color would you like?"

"I'll take the blue one."

"Your total is $16.01"

I passed the cashier a twenty-dollar bill.

The cashier handed me a red gas container and a blue lighter.

I left before getting my change.

"Ma'am, your change!" he yelled as I walked out of the door. I continued on. Collecting change was the last thing on my mind.

David's words echoed through my mind as I pumped the gasoline into the red container. *We were never in a relationship; you were never my woman. Why do you think I kept fucking around on you? I made it very clear that I don't give a fuck about you.*

"You didn't give a fuck, huh, David? I don't give a fuck, either. Like you told me, I deserved everything you did. Now, you deserve everything that's coming your way."

The red gasoline can was filled to the brim. I placed the container on the floor in my back of my car. I started my car and headed for Danielle's house. I drove in silence. I was hurt, angry, and still in shock.

David's words pierced my soul like a sharp knife jabbing at it. *We were never in a relationship; you were never my woman. Why do you think I kept fucking around on you? I made it very clear that I don't give a fuck about you.* David's voice replayed in my head. "David, you cold-hearted, fucked-up muthafucka. You ain't shit!" I screamed at the top of my lungs, sitting in the car. "You ain't shit, David. I gave you everything I had, I opened myself up to you, I let you in my home, I was there when you were down, and you have the nerve to say I ain't ever had good intentions for you! You a goddamn lie! You just used me." Thinking about it more made me realized that this shit just didn't happen overnight; this muthafucka had planned this shit and used me until he no longer needed me.

● ● ●

He never gave any fuck about me.

We were never in a relationship; you were never my woman. Why do you think I kept fucking around on you? I made it very clear that I don't give a fuck about you... David's last words continued to echo in my ears as I drove down the 15 Freeway. David got me fucked up. I turned the radio on to break the silence and drown out David's words.

I was furious, hurt, and in disbelief, but then again, there was nobody I could really be mad at but myself. How did I allow a man to drag me this low? My unfinished business was with him and would soon come to an end.

I turned the music up even louder until I couldn't feel my ears.

"This is DJ Butter Baby. Call in with your song request. I'll be spinning these records 'til 4:00 a.m., uncut and uncensored.

"This is DJ Butter Baby. Who is this?"

"Hi. My name is Jennifer, and I got a song request. Play "F.D.N." by Dreezy. I dedicate this song to my best friend, Latrice, who got her heart broken by a fuck boy who didn't deserve her love from the start. Keep your head up, queen!"

"You got it, Jenn! It's Dreez on the track."

*It's Dreez!

Fuck dat nigga, fuck dat nigga

Fuck dat nigga, fuck dat nigga

You trippin', you too quick to fall in love with niggas

That's why I get this money and I never cuff a nigga

Fuck dat nigga, fuck dat nigga

Fuck dat nigga, fuck dat nigga

Took me shopping, I ain't even had to fuck dat nigga

Fuck dat nigga, fuck dat nigga

Fuck David. As the song continued to play, I was getting more and more hyped. I was in love with an opportunist, a user, an abuser, a cheater, a liar, a man who didn't give a fuck about no one but himself. That dirty bastard; I should have listened to Ricki and cut his ass loose before I allowed him to drag me into his sick bullshit. Dreez's "F.D.N." continued to play in the background as I collected my thoughts.

"This is DJ Butter Baby, and the request line is open. The last song just played was dedicated to Latrice by best friend, Jennifer.

"Who is next up on my line with a request?"

"Hey, DJ Butter, this is Nicole."

"What's up, beautiful? What is your song request?"

""Deserve" by KenTheMan."

"You got it."

"DJ Butter, can I say one thing?"

"Sure thing, love."

"I just want to dedicate this song to every woman. Sis, know your worth. Sometimes, the person you want doesn't deserve you. Never allow a man to disrespect or mistreat you."

"Great advice to the ladies. Nicole, thanks for calling in. You got it! KenTheMan is now on the track.

♪♪♪

I don't deserve this
You don't deserve me
I don't deserve
You don't deserve
I'm way too good for you
I'm way too good for you

♪♪♪

"This DJ Butter Baby. KenTheMan went in on that track! I'm loving the Woman Empowerment Movement. All right now, I have time for one more request," the DJ said.

I made my exit off the freeway; I was less than a mile away. It was pitch dark with very few street lights on. I got off on the exit and followed the GPS's direction.

"This next track I'm going to play is, "Love the Way You Lie" by Eminem featuring Rihanna.

CHAPTER 5
Fast Forwarded

♪♪♪

Just going to stand there
And watch me burn
But's that's alright because I like the way it hurts
Just going to stand there and hear me cry.
But that's alright because I love the way you lie.
I love the way you lie.

♪♪♪

I blanked out and, within that moment, I heard the lyrics to "Love the Way You Lie" by Eminem, featuring Rihanna, playing in the back of my mind.

As I walked closer to the car, with the moon at my back, a red gas can in my left hand, and a lighter tightly enfolded in my right hand, my silhouette on the ground was keeping me company. This was the last straw and the ultimate betrayal. For once, I had no mercy, and every bit of that dissipated, right along with the many tears I'd shed over the years.

"J, please. Don't," a voice echoed behind me. "You got too much to lose. Please, just give me the lighter. You can keep the gasoline. Don't throw your whole life away. Please, J, I'm begging you. I feel your pain; I swear I do. If nobody else understands, you know I do," Monica begged. "Unfortunately, it's a cold world and people with good hearts always get hurt the most. I know, Jayla. I know that you didn't deserve any of that! But leave revenge to karma, and know that what goes around always comes back, you just have to let it go, boo. And, trust that, it's going to come back ten times worse. We love you, and this ain't it, boo. I swear this ain't it."

I took a few more steps closer to the car, clenching tighter and tighter to the red gas can.

"You will regret your decision in the morning when you wake up in jail. Think long and hard before you take any more steps closer to that car. Is this really the life you want? Is it really worth it? What will setting that car on fire change?" Monica asked one question after another. "I swear, Jayla, this is just another chapter in your life; don't let it be a life sentence. Time heals all wounds. You just have to find your healing. Your scars will eventually heal; you either allow yourself to suffer or let go of what no longer serves you."

"Tell me how to do it, Monica, because I'm on the verge of saying fuck everything, and honestly, the way I feel right now, I'm willing to risk going to jail and smiling in my mugshot," I said, as tears quickly emerged down my face, angrily thinking about taking my next step toward the car.

"Start by working out again, invest that anger into something constructive, pick up a new hobby, take cooking classes…" Monica said as she fumbled over words and ideas, hoping to convince me.

As I zoned out for a moment, Monica's voice became nothing more than a whispering wind passing by my ears. I was not trying to hear any of that shit. "This muthafucka," I said painfully, peering at the car parked in the driveway.

I closed my eyes and thought about all the people who loved me and all the people who would be without me. As I took in a deep breath, I knew this wasn't me, but the pain from betrayal would bring change to a person, and that's what had taken place. Being hurt

● ● ●

repeatedly can create a monster out of anyone, and that's exactly what I am becoming. I am tired of being loyal, tired of the disrespect, tired of the lies, tired of the betrayals, tired of turning the other cheek, I am just tired. There's no pain worse than realizing the person you were once in love with was just there to teach you a lesson.

I opened my eyes and just stared at the car. Monica's voice phased back in. "J, I know how you can heal. Put the gas can down and pick up a pen. Write, Jayla; you love to write. Find your healing in that, not behind bars. Snatch your energy back and put the focus back on yourself. Get caught up on your goals, your dreams, and your grind. You are bigger than this. This is your time to glow up. Tell your story. Free yourself, heal yourself. Remember, there is no better story than a woman who rose from the cold fucking floor she was left on to reclaim her heart and save herself," Monica said, trying to comfort the pain I am experiencing.

I immediately drop the gas can; I know Monica was right. Setting this car on fire wasn't going to change any fucking thing besides changing my home address to an inmate number. I needed to heal, and writing had always been my therapy since I was a little girl. I had a story to tell. I turned around and there was Monica. She was relieved that I had dropped the gas can.

She was walking toward me, with the moon glistening off her. I began to walk in her direction until we met in the middle of the street. She opened her arms and gave me a big comforting hug. "Write your story; don't let this break you down, you must be strong," she whispered into my ear. "You're not the first and you won't be the last to go through this. Write your story with no hesitation in the truth. Help yourself heal, be as open and transparent as you need to be. Expose the raw and real. Don't be ashamed, J. This is your truth. This is the coldest summer..."

● ● ●

As we heard sirens sounding in the distance, we knew then that it was time to go. Monica grabbed me by the hand and we quickly ran back to her car.

"I can't leave my car here," I told her.

"Don't trip, Ashton drove down here with me. Give her your keys because your ass is riding with me. I have to keep my eye on you," Monica said.

"Wait, how did you know I was here?"

"I just had a gut feeling that I would find you here, especially since you weren't answering your phone, and, unfortunately, under the circumstances, Ashton and I got here just in time."

"Wait, how did you find the address?"

Monica laughed and said, "The same way you did," and winked at me.

"Now, let's go write this story. My story is filled with broken pieces, bad decisions, and some ugly truths."

The hardest pill I had to swallow this year was learning that no matter how good to somebody you could be, and no matter how much you loved them, they could turn their back on you, and there's absolutely nothing you could do but suck it up and keep moving forward. Remember this one thing if you don't remember anything else in my story: "There will always be someone who doesn't see your worth, just don't let it be you."

✳✳✳✳✳✳✳

"Look, Jayla, I know it's painful, but now is the time you have to be mentally and emotionally strong or you're going to lose yourself and find yourself in a lot of trouble. You have to train your mind to be stronger than your emotions. You can come back from this, and trust me, he will regret it," Monica said.

"He is getting married to her, Monica. What the fuck? I trusted and loved him. I put up with so much shit and gave so much of my time and myself just to please him, and this is how it ends? Really?"

"He did not deserve you, Jayla, and my heart goes out to both you and the woman he intends to marry. Trust me, no woman deserves to be with a man that doesn't loves her. Moreover, David is a coward who runs away from his problems, one woman after another. Divine Intervention showed you exactly who he is and exposed his ugly truth to you. Unfortunately, the other woman has no clue and will discover his ugly truth on her own, and who knows, karma might just hit his ass then.

"You have to understand, Jayla, being pretty won't keep a man, having sex won't keep a man, having a baby won't keep a man. Hell, being a good woman still won't keep a man.

"The only thing that keeps a man is a man that wants to be kept. And he didn't want to be kept by you. I promise you; you dodged a bullet. He wasn't the one for you. In life, you will realize that there is a role for everyone you meet. Look, J, people come into our lives for a reason or a season; not everyone is meant to be. David was temporary. Some will test you, some will use you, some will love you, and some will teach you. It just so happened that he played all the roles and showed you his true colors. Temporary people teach permanent lessons, and he is a temporary person in your life, J."

I looked out out the passengers' side window as we made our way to the 15 Freeway going North.

"Hear me clearly, Jayla. You can come back from anything, and when you're healed and ready, the right man will come into your life. He will love you correctly. You will know what signs to be aware of, and when the right man finds you, you will know. It will be a love and happiness you have never experienced. He will pray with you, for you, and love you like a real man is supposed to love you. I truly believe that, J, regardless of the drama and heartache. Do you know that you *deserve* that? You will look back at this experience and be thankful that

● ● ●

it happened. You will even thank the man that caused you this pain. Although David did some fucked up shit, you will have to be able to forgive him so you can fully love yourself and move on. This is because when you come full circle with this, you will fully understand the reason it had to end like this.

"You're going to be okay, Jayla, I promise. Unfortunately, most women have all gone through something similar, if not worst. I can testify to that, Jayla, you know my story. At some point in our life, we've all been a good woman to the wrong man. A good woman will beak her own heart expecting an ungrateful ass man to be solid and supportive as she is.

"Tonight, you are staying over at my place," Monica demanded. "Ashton will bring your car there so you don't have to worry about that. We are here to support you and also get you get through this. We love you and we will always have your back.

"You are one of the most beautiful people I know both inside and out. I wish you could see what the rest of us see in you. You need to love the fuck out yourself, J, and put all that extra energy into yourself. It's okay to be selfish; you've already given so much to others. Now is the perfect time to pour into you to heal you. Remember that healing is realizing that nobody can take anything that you aren't supposed to lose. Not everything you love is meant to be kept. He did you a favor."

"Look at me, Jayla, just promise me you won't do anything to get yourself in trouble. No need for revenge; just sit back and wait. Those who hurt you will eventually get theirs. The best revenge is moving on being happy and let karma do the rest. No matter how much it hurts now, one day you will look back and realize it actually changed your life for the better. I don't know your pain about experiencing a miscarriage, but honey, know that God makes no mistakes. Maybe it was God's plan that you don't have a baby for that monster. You will make a great mom someday, and I know this is true because you are such a great godmother to my children.

"I've watched how you interact and act patiently with them, and the spark you have in your eyes when you see them running around. Your time will come one day, and when it does, the experience will be breathtaking. Things could have been hundred times worse, but when you're finally ready to tell your story, your testimony will touch many other people."

I looked at Monica, confused. I couldn't make any promises.

"He hurt me to the core. I was sharing my bed with the enemy this whole time. This muthafucka played me like a fool. He had this planned this the whole time and I couldn't even see it coming, or maybe I did and just over looked the obvious. I was good to this man. I held him down. I opened up my home, my heart, my body, and my soul to this man. I helped him when he was broke, hungry, and sick. When he lost his job, I was there, supporting him through it all. And now, he had the nerves to tell me he was never my man and I never had his best interest at heart, and rubbed it in by getting married. He blamed me for everything, while it was him the whole time. He played me," I said, as I wiped the tears from my eyes.

"This m-u-t-h-a-f-u-c-k-a" were the only words I could use to describe him. I sat in silence on the journey to Monica's house. A million different things were going through my head, mainly on how to get even with him. How could I have been so naive, so blinded? This is the last time this m-u-t-h-a-f-u-c-k-a will fuck me over.

"We've all played the fool at some point in our lives," Monica said. "There is no reason to blame yourself. It's not your fault, J."

I close my eyes and nod into a slight nap.

✳✳✳✳✳✳✳

"Jayla, we are home," Monica said, tapping me on the shoulder. I opened my eyes and unfastened my seat belt. "You're going to sleep in my room tonight. I want you to get some good rest if you can. I know it's a lot to digest right now; you will not go through this alone."

● ● ●

I got out of the car and followed Monica as we made our way into the house.

"Mo, can you pour me a glass of wine? I'll take whatever you've got. Let me even take the strongest drink you have. Fuck the wine, pour me a shot. I definitely can use a shot."

Monica made her way to the bar, which she kept loaded with cognac, whiskey, brandy, tequila, rum, Hennessy, vodka. She had a variety of liquor for every occasion.

Mo opened a bottle of Crystal Head Vodka, placed two shot glasses on the counter top, and poured vodka until it spilled over.

Monica sat next to me on the couch, and handed me the shot. We looked at each other, nodded, and took our shots. No chaser was needed.

"Do you need another one?" Monica asked.

"Yes, I can take one more."

Monica returned moments later, and we took another shot.

"I'll be honest, those shots helped calm my nerves a bit. Mo, if you wouldn't have come when you did, girl, I would have set that shit on fire. I probably would have stood there and watched that shit burn into ashes. And then, who knows if I would have gotten away with it—"

"Girl," Monica interrupted, "you are crazy. He ain't worth you going to jail or losing everything you worked so hard to achieve. I was serious when I told you to write your story.

"You've been through so much with this man; you allowed so much. Now, use what you've been through to be a part of your healing. You're not the only woman out there who played the fool and accepted the bullshit. A lot of us get invested too early on; we don't set boundaries, and unfortunately, that's when we realize we don't even love ourselves enough to walk away especially when they start to disrespect us or show us that they don't value us.

To move forward, the healing is all up to you. No one can do the work for you, J. No one can take the heartache and heartbreak away, and that comes with time and working on yourself esteem. No one can make you feel good about you, but you. This healing is an inside job, and it's going to require you to be completely honest with yourself. Go for therapy sessions, work on yourself, the very parts of you that make you feel like you are not worth it, or don't deserve love or to be treated right.

This is solely about you and your growth. I can't say this is going to be an easy and beautiful journey of self-love, because it probably won't be. There are days, you may even be awake and pissed the hell off, just thinking about old shits and all the shit you tolerated, but the journey is yours and no one else. You don't have to apologize for being selfish with yourself. You don't have to be careful with what write in your story and you damn sure don't have to save anyone's reputation because it's your truth and about you owning and acknowledging it. And once you do, that's when you know you're are allowing yourself to begin healing.

I'm speaking from experience, you know that. You were there when I went through my bullshit. You watched me transition from feeling broken and not feeling good enough to the woman I am today. I put that work in, Jayla. I cried a lot, prayed a lot, started to mediate. I got down to the root of my issues and I confronted them head on until they were no longer issues.

"I'm not saying it's going to happen just like that, but if you start the process you will realize that you worth so much more, you deserve so much more, and you have been settling for way less than you deserved."

"You're right, Monica. I know I deserve so much more. I didn't see my own worth. I allowed this muthafucka to manipulate and abuse me verbally and emotionally. I took all the bullshit because I thought that if I would stand by his side, I could prove to him that I was his ride or die, and the woman for him. As I see that shit didn't work, never again will a person show me who they really are and will think otherwise. I'm definitely going to believe it." I took in a deep breath

● ● ●

and exhaled. "I'm tired, Mo." I looked over to check the time and it was 3:20 a.m. in the morning.

I wiped the tears from my face. "I think I'm just going to go to bed now. We can continue in the morning."

I headed into Monica's bedroom. I paused for a moment and looked back. "Mo, thank you for saving me tonight. You are a life saver."

"Girl, you know I got you. Get you some rest. I'm going to sleep in the kids' room tonight."

"The kids are around?" I asked.

"No, they are with their dad. Ashton should be here in a few minutes with your car. So, I'm just going to wait up for her."

"Okay. Goodnight, Mo."

"Goodnight, J. Just remember it's going to be okay! Everything heals with time."

✳✳✳✳✳✳✳

As I was hoping to get some much-needed rest, I heard Monica's cell phone ringing.

"Hey, Ashton. You here?"

"Yes, I'm parking out in front right now."

"Okay, I'll open the door for you."

Monica got up off the couch and opened the door for Ashton.

"Where is she?" Ashton asked as she walked in, looking around.

"She just went to my room."

"How is she?"

"As of now, she is okay. We talked on our way here and once we got here."

"That was crazy as fuck, Monica. I ain't ever seen this side of her before. He pushed all the buttons and she went into destructive mode."

"Listen, Ashton, I need you to gather all the girls; we need to have a Sistas Circle. Jayla is going to need all the emotional support from us. I'll make us brunch in the morning, and have everyone meet here around noon. We need to keep our eyes on Jayla."

"Here are her keys."

"Yes, I definitely will be holding on to these," Monica said, taking the keys from Ashton. I know it's late. If you want to stay here tonight, you can."

"No, it's okay. I will go home and get some rest, too. I'll reach out to everyone first thing in the morning," Ashton said, walking toward the door.

Monica gave Ashton a hug. "Thanks, Ash, for coming with me."

"Girl, no problem. You know when one roll, we all roll together."

"I'll see you at noon."

"Goodnight. Please, text me to let me know you made it home safe."

"Will do, Mo."

As the front door closed, I heard Monica yawn, and what sounded like stretching, she said, "What a night!" She exhaled loudly.

Monica went into the kitchen and probably poured herself another shot. She turned off the lights and made her way to the kids' room.

"Man, I'm tired as hell," she said, as she walked past the bedroom door.

As I lay in the bed, I tossed and turned all through the night, replaying every scenario in my head. I should have left then, in the very beginning when he got Raquel pregnant. Instead, I was naive. Hell, I should have left after he told me I was going to be a single parent. I was the fool, I was blind, I was so caught up trying to fix his shit, when in reality, everything was already broken beyond repair. I made myself look desperate for a relationship, but that still doesn't give this muthafucka the right to just treat me *so* fucked up.

All the could've, would've, and should've didn't even matter because I didn't do anything, and now, it's too late.

I continued to toss and turn until I became restless and fell asleep.

✳✳✳✳✳✳✳

"Good morning, J," Monica said, peeking through the door. "Did I wake you?"

"No, you didn't. I've been awake for a while." I looked over at the window to see the sunlight peeking through the blinds. I grabbed my cell phone—it is 9:15 a.m.

"How do you feel this morning?" Monica asked.

"To be honest, I don't even know. I feel numb."

Monica made her way to her king-sized bed and lay down across from me.

"I mean, I knew Danielle was in the picture. I just didn't know how serious they were, especially since he was still living in my house. When I would ask him about her whenever I saw her call his phone, he would tell me he didn't give fuck about her and she didn't mean anything to him or she was a nobody, and I shouldn't put too much focus on what they got going on and worry about our relationship because it's nothing. I constantly believed his lies. I felt so stupid for staying and trying to make it work."

"Listen, Jayla, you have been through enough abuse. Don't beat yourself up. You're not stupid, you were in love and sometimes love can be blinding.

"It happens, unfortunately, that almost every woman has experienced something that have caused them a great ordeal of pain or betrayal. I didn't believe love is blind until I got over my ex. I thought about all the red flags I ignored, the bullshit I put up with, and the times my gut feeling were right but I choose to convince myself I was just being crazy. When we fall in love, we only see what we want to see and that's what makes it hard to walk away at times. We fall in love with the idea of who someone can become, forgetting who they are. Not everyone will live up to their potential. You fought

• • •

84

hard, cried, and really tried; you were never stupid. If anyone was stupid, it was definitely David. My ex-husband taught me that no matter how good of a woman you are, you'll never be good enough for the wrong man. He was just the wrong man, and you held on just a little too long.

"But, it's okay, you will find yourself again. Now, you just need to take the time and energy, and focus on yourself. Be yourself, boo! That's how you bounce back.

"You should really consider writing your story, J."

"Who the hell is going to read my story? I had every opportunity to pack his shit up and kick to the curb, but didn't."

"Listen, some women are stronger than others, but that doesn't mean your story isn't worth reading. What you experienced can help the next woman find the courage and strength she needs to leave a similar situation. People write love songs, sad songs, songs about having affairs all the time. And guess what, people still sing along. You're just writing an extended version of it. One day, you will tell your story about how you overcame this battle you went though and God will send you the exact people who need to hear your story. Just consider it, Jayla. You will know when the time is right for you to start."

"Do I tell everything, Mo?" I paused. "I mean, you know almost everything."

"That's entirely up to you, J, on how vulnerable and transparent you want to get. Your whole experience is a learning experience. This whole situation is fucked up, but at some point, you can turn it around and change the narrative.

"Yes, David hurt you, used you, and betrayed you, but he also showed you the importance of loving yourself and setting healthy boundaries. One thing is for sure, you will never again tolerate anyone treating you poorly just because you love them.

"Danielle isn't getting the prize. If you really think about it, J, while he was planning a life with her, he was still sleeping with you. That means he was cheating on her and he has already fucked up. She will be walking in your shoes, sooner or later."

"I've invited some of the girls over for brunch today, just to show you some love and support. I hope you don't mind."

"I don't mind, Monica. I need to be surrounded by love."

"They should be here around noon, so, get yourself together."

"Okay, Mo."

Monica got up and walked out of the bedroom, closing the door behind her.

"Siri, set alarm for one hour."

I threw the blankets over my head and went back to sleep.

"To hell with you, David. You low down muthafucka," I said as I closed my eyes for a much-needed nap.

CHAPTER 6
The Circle of Truth

M onica's doorbell rang.
"Who is there?"

"Ashton. Open up."

Monica opened the door and greeted Ashton with a bottle of wine and hug.

"Where's Jayla?" Ashton inquired.

"She is still in the room."

"How's she taking it?"

"She is taking it quite well actually. However, all she wants to do is sleep. We spoke again this morning. One thing for sure is that she wasn't talking about setting anything else on fire. So, we are making progress."

"Okay good. Does she know about the brunch?"

"Yes, I mentioned it to her this morning. I'm sure she'll be out when she is ready."

"I spoke to Keisha. She said she was coming. Girl, I told my auntie, Debrah, what happened and she insisted on coming to the brunch. I sent Nicole a text message; she will also be here."

"Okay, good. I'm just about done cooking," Monica responded.

"It smells good in here. What are you cooking?"

"Salmon croquets, fried catfish, eggs, and homestyle potatoes. I cut up some watermelon and strawberries. Now, we are just waiting for the homemade biscuits to be done."

"I forgot you knew how to throw down in the kitchen."

"Yes, I do my thang in the kitchen. You know my momma taught all her kids how to cook."

"Hi, y'all," I said, walking into the living room.

Ashton walked over to give me a hug.

"Thank you for bringing my car last night, Ashton."

"Girl, no problem. How are you?"

"I'm okay. I mean, shit happens." I shrugged. "Life goes on. People come and people go, people disappoint you. Hell, if you let them, they'll use you and still not give a fuck about you. But, you know, I'm okay."

Monica and Ashton looked at me, and then at each other. They knew I was not okay.

Ashton hugged me again. "It's okay not be okay, Jayla. You're human and you have feelings. It's okay to cry, be angry. Just know we're here; we got you, we love you, and we are going to get you through this."

Monica's doorbell rang again.

"Who is it?"

"It's Keisha. Mo, open up."

Monica opened the door and greeted Keisha with a hug.

✳✳✳✳✳✳✳

"Where's left eye?" Keisha asked out loud. Keisha walked over and gave me a hug. "Next time, call me. I'll ride with you," Keisha whispered in my ear. "I don't know all the details, but I know one damn thing, that muthafucka is disrespectful. I don't wish bad upon anybody, but you will reap what you sow in life. You don't treat people like shit and live a happy life."

"You're right, Keisha, I was good to David. I wasn't perfect, but I tried my best to be the woman for him. In the beginning, he would always tell me how controlling his ex was and how she always gave him a hard time. He made her out to be the villain and him the victim—"

"Listen, sis," Keisha interrupted. "Every story a man tells you about his past relationship and how his ex was a crazy toxic bitch, just know that the ex is him. He's the crazy toxic bitch."

"I see that now. I was trying *so* hard to be different, not to follow in her footsteps. He would constantly remind me of how controlling she was. I didn't want be controlling, I didn't want to push him away.

"You know, I blame a lot of it on me. I fell fast for him, gave him the key to my place in four months of knowing him. He was living at his cousin's house, sleeping on the couch after his relationship ended with his child mother. And when he would stay the night, he would make reference to how comfortable he felt lying in bed next to me every night.

"I was in love with him and we were spending every day together. I didn't see it being a problem. I mean, it wasn't like I told him he could move in, it was a second option to lay his head after work instead of him taking that long drive to his cousin's house. But eventually, he would come over after work every day, he would be there on weekends, too. More and more of his belongings began to surface. But I didn't mind the company because we had such a good time while we were together. For a moment, I thought I found Mr. Right.

"David didn't make a lot of money after child support. So, I never asked him to contribute in the house.

"That shit backfired! The whole three years he lived with me, he never paid a dime toward rent or any of the bills. He lived off me. At first, I thought I was helping him save money so he could catch up on his bills and pay his attorney. I'm even embarrassed to say this; I gave him $1,500 to pay his attorney for his child custody case. I mean, that was my way of showing him I had his back. So, not only was I letting him live with me free, I was also helping him with some of the bills that he complained about. It all came from a place of love. Even when his car broke down every day, I would take him to work in the morning at 5:00 a.m. and pick him up by 2:30 p.m. on my off days. It would take thirty to forty-five minutes to get him to work due to a lot of traffic most days going east. It would take me an hour and ten minutes to get home because it was so much traffic going west. And the days I worked, I would let him use my car and I would take Uber to work because my job was literally only ten minutes' drive away from the house. I would take Uber to work and he would pick me up when I got off by 8:30 p.m. We shared one car for about five months until David got himself a new Durango truck.

"I was trying to show David, in every possible way, that I had his back. There were times he wouldn't appreciate my efforts. He would tell me anybody could have done that: 'You ain't the first woman I've had who has taken me to work when my car broke down.' I won't lie, that made me feel bad sometimes, but I didn't express my feelings to him. I still tried to be there, a team player. I would wash his personal clothes and his work clothes every week, cook him dinner every night. Some days, I even made lunch for work.

"I truly thought I was being a good woman to him. I had his back in more than one way. I would pray for him every night. I would ask God to ease his load and give him peace, to protect him. I didn't know all the burdens he carried because he only shared with me what he wanted me to know, but I would pray for him. If he needed anything and I had it, I would share. I wasn't selfish.

"I remember this one particular time I knew David was stressed about cash; he had an outstanding ticket and they suspended his license. He got this ticket way before he knew me and I had no idea his license was suspended until he told me. Since he was going to the child custody court, he needed to have his license reinstated in order to drive his son around. The judge made it a court order that by the next court date he needed to have his license. David walked around the house dismayed and after constantly asking what was wrong, he finally told me. when I asked him how much he has saved, I learned that he had nothing saved. Every time I would ask him what he was doing with his money, his reply always was that paying bills took all his money. I loaned David $600 to get his license reinstated before his court date!

"Looking backing now, I know exactly what he was doing with his money, he was spending his money on other women. That's why his ass was broke. But I didn't see it then until now.

"I'll never keep giving to a man for the sake of trying to prove that I have his back, because he will only take advantage of it.

"David would always tell me, once he got his business off the ground, he would take care me. He would tell me that he would buy me the biggest house, get me the most beautiful boat, and we would take family trips every summer. David painted this beautiful picture of our future together, even though I saw the cracks in the frame. I didn't mind helping David when he needed that an extra support. I wanted to be that good woman that held her man down when he was struggling. I believed in David.

Looking back, I was a fool in love with a boy. And I was foolish to keep giving foolishly. The last most recent event was when his Durango black truck got repossessed while he was at work.

"I got a phone call while I am at work and it's from David.

'J, I have a problem. They just repossessed my truck and I'm at work.

'Okay. What do you need me to do? I can't leave work to get you.'

'Can you send me an Uber to pick me up from work and take me to my cousin's house?'

'Sure, I got you. I can do that.'

'Then, after you get off, you can just pick me up from there.'

● ● ●

'Okay. We can figure something out from there.'

"So, I sent an Uber when he got off. After my long twelve hours shift, I left work to pick David up from his cousin's house in Harbor City.

"I watched David lie about how his car broke down and he towed it to the shop.

"David was a very good lair, and I mean very good. I would have believed him if I didn't know the truth myself.

'J, I have to work tomorrow, can you take me to work? I just have two more days of work this week to figure something out.'

'How far back do you owe on your car note?'

'I owe at least three months.'

'Three months, David? What are you doing with your money?'

'I don't want to talk about it right now, Jayla. Will you be able to take me to work tomorrow or not?'

'Yeah, I'll take you, David.'

"I was already burnt out with the commute. We've been down this road before. And to be honest, I really didn't want to be the one constantly taking him to work every day, especially now, since he was broke and they repossessed his truck."

'I'm going to call around, Jayla. I'm going to see if my father can loan me some money, I'll even ask a few friends. I have to do something quick because every day they have it, they will charge a storage fee.'

'How much exactly do you owe, David?'

'With the bank payment and the tow fee, in total, I owe $1,284.45.'

'Damn, David.'

"I was completely puzzled on what David did with his money. David worked five days a week, and sometimes, overtime. He had a decent pay. He wasn't paying any bills here, but the only response he gave was that he was using his money to catch up on his bills, and that's why he was broke.

"The next day, David reached out to everyone he knew and came back empty-handed. That was the story he told me and I believed. So, me being nice again, I opened up my purse and got David's car back. David was very much appreciative; he promised he would pay back every dime and would pay me some of my money back on payday, which was on a few days. Once again, he fed me the line that he would take care of me once he got his business off the ground and pay me every dime back.

"Well, that was on a Tuesday. Payday Friday came and David didn't offer to pay anything. 'I promise, baby, next payday, I got you.' That was all he said.

"Valentine's Day came; David left for work in the morning. Before he left, he reminded me he wouldn't be coming straight home because it was his visitation day with his son. I thought, maybe after work, David would have something planned for me, especially since I just dropped a shot load of cash to get his Durango back. Well Ladies, David never came home that night. I called his phone several times, and nothing. He didn't even have the time to text me back nor did I receive a 'Happy Valentine's Day' from his ass.

"David didn't answer his phone 'til morning.

'Where the fuck were you, David?' I asked, infuriatedly.

'Baby, I was at my cousin's house. I fell asleep there. It got late dropping off my son and I came here to crash.'

'David, yesterday was Valentine.'

'Baby, you know I don't really celebrate Valentine. That's not my thing.'

'No David, that doesn't even seem legit. You know all women love Valentine.'

'I'm sorry, baby, I'll make it up to you. I'll take you to dinner tonight. I'll make it up to you, J, I promise.'

"I had a gut feeling David was lying through his teeth. I knew, but still remained loyal to him, even after he showed me bullshit.

• • •

"David always had a way of turning the tables on me, saying he couldn't trust me, and that he thought I was cheating on him, and if I were doing what I ought to, I wouldn't have to worry about outsiders. I couldn't see that he was just manipulating me, trying to get the attention off of him.

"But I continued with David, tried to fix my appearance, wore sexier clothes, made sure I kept my hair up. I wanted to look more attractive for him. I questioned everything about me as if I was the problem.

"David would disappear on the weekends and surfaced back on Mondays after work. It started to become a pattern that I got used to.

"And every time I would confront David, he would complain that I was just like his ex, trying to control him. 'David, I can't do this anymore, I'm tired. I think it's time for you to go. Something in my gut tells me that you and Danielle have something on.'

'You just like everyone other woman I've been with; you are turning your back on me. See, I knew you weren't different.' David's guilt trap always worked.

"This past October, David lost job. He called me to come home, and he told me they fired him. Immediately, I updated his resume and started helping him fill out job applications online. I mean, we woke and went to sleep filling out applications. Even the weekends he disappeared; I was still filling out applications. I took him to multiple interviews because he didn't have any gas in his truck. I was there for him way more than he was ever there for me.

"I'll tell y'all a secret. One of the last few times I saw David, he came home looking depressed.

'Why are you so depressed?'

'I think I'm not hirable,' he said, as he laid across the couch. 'I went on all these interviews and no one has called me back.'

'You'll get a job,' I said. 'We won't stop putting in applications until you do.'

'Jbaby, when I do get a job, I'm going to take you on vacation anywhere you want to go and I'm going to take you to your favorite restaurant. This time, I'm more determined to get my business up and going on. Baby, we are going to have a good future together. Thank you for helping me. I appreciate you.'

"The next day, David disappeared again.

"A few days passed; I didn't hear from David. I tried to reach him, but he never returned my calls.

"While in the grocery store, I came across an old friend of mine by the name of Sam. We had small talk, but during our conversation, he told me that he changed jobs and now he worked at a warehouse in Buena Park as the hiring manager assistant.

'Sam, I know someone looking for a job. Are they hiring?'

'How well do you know this person?'

'He is my boyfriend. He recently lost his job, and it's been hard out here for him.'

'Look, I can get him in. I just need you to email me his resume and have him or you fill out an application online. I'll talk to the hiring manager, Allison, about him. He will still need to go through an interview process, background, and drug test. If he passes the major requirements, I'll get him in.'

'Thank you *so* much, Sam. It was truly a blessing to see you today.'

'Here's my business card, Send the resume to my email address.'

'Sam, do me one last favor. Don't mention that you know me or I was the plug. I want him to think he got the job himself.'

'I got it, Jayla. A man and its ego.'

'Right, Sam.'

'He should be thankful that he has a woman looking out for him.'

'Yeah, you are right about that, Sam.'

'I'll fill out everything tonight.'

'Great. And I'll pull it and give it to the human resource manager tomorrow.'

'Thank you again.'

● ● ●

'You're very welcome, Jayla.'

"I got David the job he is at now, and still doesn't know.

"The very next day, Sam reached out and told me he called David for an interview.

"I was so excited and thought David was going to call and share the good news about the interview or even that he was offered a job.

"Days passed and not one word from David. I reach out to Sam again asking for an update. 'David got hired,' he said.

"I reached out, but my calls went unanswered; sent text messages, nothing. And finally, David texted me.

'Why are you now so concerned about me finding job, it's not like you were helping. I haven't seen one email receipt in my email of you recently filling out applications.

'Excuse me, David, I've been helping since the day you told me you lost your job.'

'Yeah, you did, but what have you done for me lately?'

I don't need you anymore saying you are going to help me, and not follow through. I need a woman who is going to be a person of her word and be there during my toughest times.'

'David, I've been putting applications in.'

'I haven't seen anything in my email.'

'But, I have, David. I have.'

"David never responded back after that text message. And I didn't bother to send another one to explain myself.

"It was days late after that conversation that I got a phone call from David.

'Listen, J, I'm getting married. I can never see you again.'

'What do you mean by you are getting married, David? You were just here with me.'

'Jayla, no man ain't going to want a woman he can't trust.'

'What are you taking about, David?'

'I haven't forgotten about you following me from work.'

• • •

'David, that was year one of our relationship when I knew you were fucking around on me.'

'Let's getting something clear, Jayla. We were never in a relationship; you were never my woman. Why do you think I kept fucking around on you? I made it very clear that I don't give a fuck about you. You deserved everything I did to you. You never had my back or had any good intentions for me. You are just like every other woman I've dealt with.'

"And that's when I wanted to fuck up his world; that fucked up muthafucka! He accused me of cheating, blaming me! It was him! I always bent backwards for that man, and he had the nerve to tell me that bullshit. I am not even mad that he is getting married to Danielle. Fuck it! What pissed me off was how he left. He got his damn nerves talking about me following him to work.

"One year into our relationship, or whatever the fuck it was, when I found out about Raquel, I became more aware when things don't sit right. So, this particular day, he was leaving for work, but he took extra clothes with him. That day, he worked from 2:30 p.m. to 10:30 p.m. When I asked where he was going after work, he said his cousin had a birthday dinner he was going to attend. That didn't sit right in my soul.

"He left for work and I called Denise and asked if I could use her car that evening. I texted David by 7 p.m., and asked if he was coming home after for dinner. He said, 'No. I actually left work early because I got a headache. I'm actually at my cousin, Shawn's house, resting before the dinner.

'Do you need anything baby?' I asked.

'No bae, I'm good. But, goodnight. I'll see you tomorrow.'

"My gut told me he was lying. So, I pulled up to his job at 10:00 p.m., thirty minutes before he got off of work. And there was his car in the parking lot. I read over our text just to make sure I didn't miss anything. It was clearly written that he left work and went to his cousin's house.

● ● ●

"Twenty minutes later, David walked out of the warehouse, and I parked across. I followed him because it was very clear David had somewhere to be. It was all just a lie. Twenty minutes of following him, he saw that I was in Denise's car because but her windows were not tinted.

"He called me, and asked me where I was. I asked him the same question again and he told me it was not my business and I should answer his question. That turned into a whole other situation. David later confessed that he was going to meet some woman off of Plenty of Fish..."

Keisha stopped me. "No, sis, fuck him. I see exactly why you went Left Eye. That's a cold muthafucka. He said what? That you'll never see him again? Shit! My ass would be petty. How much did you loan him over the years and he never paid back?"

"Maybe like $3500," I replied.

"I would take his ass to small claims court and get my money back. I would walk in that courtroom with the biggest smile on my face, just waving. And let him bring his wife, 'cause I would be spilling all the tea. I bet when she finds out who her husband really is, this muthafucka would learn that day.

"I tell you, he got this much coming. Karma is bitch, and nothing good is going to come to him. All he did was string you along until he got in good with Danielle. People don't abandon people they love; they abandon people they are using."

"Ain't that much love in the world to keep letting somebody disrespect you, Jayla, " Ashton added.

"I've been hurt before, Jayla," Keisha shared. "I know what it feels like. Now I don't take shit from anybody. Lorenzo's ass taught me that lesson. I loved his dirty drawers and I kept giving excuses for him. Every time he would cheat, I would think I was the reason, thinking maybe I wasn't giving him enough attention, pretty enough for him, or fucking him right or enough. I looked at myself as the reason for him to constantly cheat on me. It never crossed my mind that he cheated because he wanted to.

"I remember when I finally caught Lorenzo cheating, and that was the day I had enough and snapped. And to be completely honest, I was never the same woman since.

"It was the summer of 2015. Lorenzo and I made plans to spend time together that weekend. Saturday morning came; I called Lorenzo, but he didn't answer. I didn't trip because I assumed maybe he was still sleep or at the gym. I ran my errands and noticed a few hours went by and he haven't called me back, I sent him a text message asking if he was okay. I waited for the response, and still, no response. So, I continued on with my day. I remember I had on my gym clothes that day.

"The gym was on the way to Lorenzo's house. So, as I proceeded to the gym, I drove past Lorenzo's place and saw his car in the driveway; not just his car only, but there was another car I didn't recognize in his driveway, a lemon green Ford Focus to be exact. I stopped right in front of his house and called him. Still no response. I got out the car and headed toward his house. I heard music coming from his backyard. Lorenzo didn't tell me he was a having party today, I thought. I walked up toward the backyard and opened his backyard gate, and then *boom!*

Shit unfolded. It was Lorenzo and some woman in the pool together. I screamed, 'Lorenzo! Lorenzo!'

"He didn't hear me due to the music, but she did. She got up so quick out the pool.

'Baby, baby, baby, where are you going?' He questioned her. 'We are just getting started.'

"She looked in my direction and that's when Lorenzo saw me. I stood there, with my arms folded across my chest.

'What the fuck is going on?' I said. 'Who the fuck is she, Lorenzo?'
'Baby, I can explain,' he said, sputtering.
"I already knew whatever would follow next was going to be a lie.

'We were just chilling.'

I looked over at the woman. She was a brown skin, thick chick. She was clueless. She stood there, drying herself off.

'I'm tired, Lorenzo. I can't take this shit anymore! Every time I turn around, you fuck around on me. Fuck this shit, I'm tired. I don't deserve this.'

"I turned to baby girl. 'Look, I think it's best you leave now. This doesn't have anything to do with you and you don't want to be in the middle of this.'

"She paused, wiping herself down and looked directly at Lorenzo. It must have been a twenty-second pause of her starting at him.

"Lorenzo gave her a head nod, and she grabbed her belongings and headed to the gate to leave.

'Oh, fuck no!' I said shouted. 'I'm done with this bullshit. Lorenzo, I hope you told her you are giving away herpes.'

"It was at that very moment, hearing myself, that I knew I what had to truly be done. I was constantly playing Russian roulette with my life. Lorenzo already gave me herpes, what could be next? It was clear it would always be one woman after the next. He knew I would take him back time after time. But this time, I was through.

"Lorenzo sat in the pool. 'Come on, Keisha. Don't be mad. I just wanted to have some fun. You know I love you.'

'Fuck you, Lorenzo, I'm done.'

'You always say you're done, but you always come right back, Keisha.'

'Today is a new day, and I am choosing myself this time.'

"And that was the day I left, Jayla. I never went back. He tried to contact me a few times. After a few attempts to reach me, I blocked his calls. He came by my house a dozen times, and each time I wouldn't answer the door. And the very last time he came, I told him if he'd come by one more time, I was going to call the police and obtain a restraining order. Since then, he never returned!

● ● ●

"Looking back at that experience, I was so busy trying to make something work with someone no matter how much it was hurting me. I was so consumed with not wanting to let go to the extent that I forgot that the point of being with someone was to be happy. Why hold to misery? But I did, 'cause I never had someone to show me what real love was, and he showed me just enough to stay and also taught me enough to leave, but at the end, it was wasted time in my life and I'll never do it again. I'm just so thankful that I was able to find the strength to walk away."

"Jayla, just know, eventually, it does get better," Ashton stated without any sort of explanation. "One day, you will realize that you're no longer upset, you're no longer mad, hurt, or bothered by the things that took so much of your energy and thoughts. You will find yourself in a peaceful place and you will enjoy the feeling. You will be happy that everything happened the way it did.

"Moving forwarded Jayla, you have to love yourself more than anyone else. I want you to level up unapologetically and intentionally. When you start seeing your worth, you'll find it harder to stay around people who don't. Even your taste in people will change when you learn to love yourself."

"Great advice," Monica said. "You are correct. Women need to learn to love themselves first. You are important. Your mental health is important and it is the key to your happiness. We have stop giving life to dead situations and stop staying in toxic and painful relationships. Sometimes, it's just better to be hurt for a moment than forever."

I was lost in our conversation that I didn't realize the other ladies have arrived.

"This is true. Hi, Jayla. I am Debrah, Ashton's auntie. She told me what happened and I insisted that I come and share my story with you. We need more women willing to say, 'I've been there and I'm here for you. You can always talk to me without fear of any judgment,' to remind one another we are not alone.

"Y'all so young and beautiful, tolerating bullshit that you don't have to. Please, don't waste your youth on a man that refuses to treat you or love you right. Don't settle or continue to settle; time flies so fast after you start losing yourself. One day, you will blink and you will be fifty with low self-esteem, regretting not leaving sooner. This was me twenty-six years ago. I lost myself loving a man who was never good for me in the first place. But at that time, I did what I thought would keep him faithful and keep him home. Back then, my self-esteem was shot to hell; I was being lied to, cheated on, and abused in every possible way. I found out that he was sleeping with women in my very own building and women whom I thought were my friends. After thinking about killing him for days, I decided against it and decided to take my life back, I finally found myself again, fought to believe in myself, and understand that I was worth it and deserved better. I learned my worth, I left him twenty years ago and never looked back. I'm proud to say I raised our children as a single mom and they are wonderful adults with wonderful lives. We as women have to stop staying in unhappy situations to prove how loyal we are. it's not worth your mental health. We have to learn to love ourselves first and that we don't deserve to be treated with disrespect. We have to learn how not to lose ourselves in loving the wrong man and ignoring the red flags."

"I've been there. Hi, ladies, I'm Jackie, Debrah's friend," she says as she waives. "You can suck his dick, throw it back, handle the back shots, support his dream, never give up the pussy to anyone but him, text him 'be safe have fun' every time he leaves the house, ask him if he ate, how his day was, be loyal, show him off, and I guarantee you he's still going to cheat. Five years ago, I experienced my first heartbreak. I was with Kevin for six years. And then, out of nowhere, he ended the relationship. I thought we were happy."

"Why did you and Kevin end the relationship?" I asked.

She laughed almost painfully. "One day he loved me, the next day he didn't. Strange, isn't it? How fast someone's feelings can change

● ● ●

102

and then there's nothing you can do but accept it. I tried after he ended the relationship to understand what went wrong and how it could be fixed because I was still in love with Kevin. The break up came suddenly and blind-sided me. I was devastated and tried to come up with every solution to fix whatever was broken, but Kevin left with no explanation.

"But then, an act of faith stepped in. I was driving along Long Beach blvd, and I saw Kevin and a pregnant woman holding hands, coming out of the store. I immediately busted a U-turn; I couldn't believe what I just saw. I pulled over right in front of his car before they got it in.

'Kevin!' I said loudly. 'Really?'

"The young pregnant woman asked Kevin who I was.

'Baby, get in the car, I'll handle it,' he said.

'Baby?' I questioned. 'So, she is who you left me for? Wait, you got another woman pregnant while we were together, Kevin. You were cheating on me.'

'I'm sorry, Jackie, I didn't mean for you to find out like this. Yes, is she pregnant with my child. That's why I couldn't be with you anymore. I wanted a family and you couldn't give me that. So when she got pregnant, it was only right that I end my relationship with you. I never meant to hurt you. I just didn't know how to tell you.'

'Kevin, we could have had kids. We could have tried IVF. You didn't have to go out and cheat me. I loved you, Kevin.'

'I'm sorry, Jackie. I have to go now.' Kevin drove off, and that was the last time I saw him.

"From that experience I learned, 'Chased love is not love.' If you have to run after it, talk it into staying, remind it of your value, fight alone for the both of you, issue ultimatums, or test it, it's not happiness, it's not fair, it's not healthy; the only thing it is is a waste of your time. If they want to leave, let them go. What's the hardest for a woman isn't losing him, it's forgiving herself for falling in love with

● ● ●

his potential, knowing damn well she saw the warning signs and inconsistencies."

"I am Diamond, Jackie's daughter. Everyone has been saying you have to "love yourself enough." This has nothing to do with self-love. This is about trying to show a man, that's not worth it, what you are willing to do for him so he can love you the way you love him. The problem is, we don't see who he really is until after we have given our hearts to them, put our all into them; then, it hurts like hell to walk away. So, you are stuck with, 'If I leave him, it's going to hurt' or 'If I stay, it's going to hurt, but at least, he is still here.' Every woman has or will go through this, at least once. You can't tell a woman when to let a man go; she has to reach her breaking point and only then will she be strong enough to walk away, and most importantly, stay away!

"A lot of times, when a woman leaves a long term relationship, the man's very first thoughts are: 'She has found someone else,' 'How could she do this,' 'All these years together,' and so much more. But what men don't think about is all the times she went to sleep feeling like crap and crying, and how he made promises he would change, but never did. Good dick and lies will have a woman waste three to seven years of her life, but when she finally decides to leave, she won't leave because she has found someone new; she would leave for herself.

"Ladies, we are not rehabilitation centers for men. It's not our job to fix them, change, re-parent them, or even raise them. We talk about women having daddy issues and needing for a man to be around. Why don't we mention men having mommy issues and needing love from multiple women to fill that void?

"The maturity of picking a man that's worth your heart will come with time and life experience. Some people are too emotionally damaged to love and some people are too emotionally damaged to walk away. For whoever is still finding their strength to leave, when you do, it's really the best feeling in the world."

"I totally get what you're saying, Jackie. I'm Nicole, Jackie's friend. I've been there. I had an ex who wrong me. I gave my everything to him and it was a bad breakup. During our relationship, I was abused mentally, emotionally, and physically. I got tired of walking on eggs shells, tired of taking the blame; he would blame me for everything. If I would wash his clothes and they didn't smell like the detergent, he would start an argument. If I didn't call him and let him know I was leaving the house, he would accuse me of cheating. No matter what I did, it literally ended up in us having an argument. Some people are great manipulators, they can lie, cheat, treat you badly, and somehow manage to make it all seem like it's your fault. I got tired of being voiceless and quieting my voice, thinking twice before I spoke. It became exhausting. When I finally decided to leave, that's when the Devil appeared. My ex, Paul, did what he could to make my life miserable. I won't get into much details because it still affects me. But what I want to tell you, Jayla, even though David is getting married, count it as a blessing. You were holding on to someone that wasn't holding on to you. He was a user, and you don't need any leech attached to you.

"Consider going to therapy, redirect your focus back to you, check all your relationships, and learn the difference between connection and attachment. Connection gives you power, but attachment sucks the life out of you. We become attached to be people to fill a void within ourselves or because of low self-esteem, lust, fear, and loneliness. Not all ties in your life belong there. Some are just replacing the love you haven't been giving yourself.

"One day, you will come across someone who you may take interest in, but take your time to heal before jumping into someone new. I made that mistake.

"I thought I was okay to get into another relationship, but I was wrong. When I got into this new one, I had a lot of issues including PTSD, depression, and anxiety, that at the time I didn't know, I lashed out and said a lot of mean things to my man. I sat down with my him and talked to him. I told him that if he wanted to leave, he could. He didn't have to stay, but he decided to stay with me and work with me with my issues. I got into therapy and it made a big difference in my life and in my mental health. I appreciate Brandon, he stayed with me through my healing process. I was fortunate to have someone else there to help me pick up the pieces. A few years later, Brandon asked me to marry him. We are blessed with twin girls now.

"You must know how valuable you are and know your worth. I see to many women put their worth in the hands of a man; it's dangerous and could make a major impact in your life. You give him the power to do as he pleases because you allow it to happen. No person should ever have you lying in bed in the middle of the night crying, and questioning your self-worth. I'm speaking from experience. I didn't want my girls to grow up not knowing their worth. I took time with myself so I would be able to lead by examples because I knew I had four little eyes watching my every move. I show my girls what confidence looks like. Now, I am so thankful that their father is a wonderful example of a man. He sets the bar high, and I truly hope that as they grown into themselves, they will make the right decisions.

"I don't know who else in this room is still struggling to learn their self-worth is still holding on to someone or something that you know isn't good for you, and yet, you still make excuses. Just know, you are worth every ounce of love; it's okay to let go and start over, and over and over. You worth it; don't believe the lies. If someone ever told you weren't good enough, I'm reminding you, you are good enough and always will be.

"Jayla, you have to look in the mirror and say fuck this shit. Smile and keep it pushing. I know it's easier said than done, but abuse is never okay. You have to learn being okay and walking away. You cannot continue to enable someone who hurts you, disrespects you, and treats you like shit. You've worked too hard to get to where you are in life."

I look around the room and I am so appreciative of every woman there sharing her story. We've all experienced a similar story at one point in our lives. This was my first experience and I pray my last.

● ● ●

Even though I didn't have the strength to walk away from David, listening to every woman's story here has given me the strength to deep dig and find my healing.

"Ladies, brunch is ready," Monica announced. "I truly want to thank everyone who showed up this afternoon."

I walked over to the radio and turn it on. Inayah Iamis' new single, "Best Thing" plays in the background.

♪♪♪

I thought I found love
But you ain't shit (no)
Gave you a space in my heart
But you ain't fit (no noo)
And it hurts but I let it
I let it cause I needed that pain
But I wanted to feel it
Cause it'll teach me not
To go back there again

♪♪♪

● ● ●

CHAPTER 7
Cell Phone

I picked up David's old cell phone that had been in his duffle bag. I've never had a desire to go through his phones because I knew what I might find.

David left me with no closure; he just told me he would never see me again and that he was getting married.

I've tolerated his cheating behavior.

I powered on David's old phone, and there was a picture of David and Danielle on his screensaver, kissing her on the cheek and she was just smiling.

Danielle was a fair-skinned older woman, possibly in her late forties. Her smile was warm and inviting. She was a beautiful woman, standing at his shoulder level, and she had to be about five-six.

I began to go through David's text messages. The first tread was of him and Danielle.

Danielle: Baby, I love you so much.

David: I love you too, baby. I can't wait to get this business off the ground, because when I do, I'm going to take care of you, buy you the biggest house and a G-wagon, and take you on trips around the world.

Danielle: Thank you, baby. I'll always support your dreams and help you in any way I can. I love you, David. Being in a relationship with you has been a dream come true. I am so thankful to have a man like you in my life.

David: Baby, I've never had a woman make feel like you do. And for that, I'm going to give you the world, I promise.

And you know what else, I like the way you take this dick. You take it, baby, you take it!

Danielle: I love you soo much, David.

David: I love you too, girl. I'll hit you back later.

The next text thread, on the same day, was from me.

Jayla: Hey, baby. Hope your day is going well?

David never responded to my text message

The next text was from Alice, on the same day.

Alice: Hey, baby, I miss you in my bed.

David: I miss being in your bed, too. I'm horny. What are you doing tonight?

Alice: Nothing, come through. My son is going to his father's.

David: I'll be there. Just hit me up when he leaves and I'll be on my way, baby.

Alice: Okay, baby. I'll wear that lingerie that you like.

David: Oh yeah, baby!! I like that shit, Girl! I'm giving you all this dick.

Francis: Hey, baby. Hope you are having a wonderful day? I really enjoyed our date yesterday. You're such a gentleman.

David: I enjoyed myself, too. You're a great dancer. If you free this Saturday night, I would like to take you out again.

Francis: I would like that.

David: Great. See you then.

• • •

Maria: I miss you so much David. I don't want the baby anymore; I just want you.

David: I'll be over later.

The more I scrolled these text messages, the more women I found. David was sleeping with about ten to twenty women. The very last text I saw was from Raquel.

Raquel: You're still mad at me, David?

David: No, I'm not mad at you. I'm just disappointed in you.

Raquel: I'll make it up to you, David. Right now, I'm sick. You know what I miss the most was when I was pregnant and had morning sickness, you took good care of me. I miss that, David.

David: I had you.

Raquel: Yes, you did. I miss fucking you. You are so nasty. You used to put your tongue everywhere, and I loved it...

I paused, unable to continue reading. When I was pregnant, David didn't take care of me. He didn't give a fuck, not one. I went to my first doctor's appointment by myself, and even when I started bleeding, David wasn't concerned.

I then went through David's duffle bag. I founded six motel key cards and hotel receipts that read, *For 2 guests*. I also found other receipts from Imperial Suites. I even found notes from Danielle: *I met you, liked you, and fell in love with you; so, I'm keeping you. I love you, baby. Have a wonderful day at work. – love, Danielle.* I'd be willing to bet that he wasn't at the motel with Danielle. She had her own place to fuck.

I went through the photo albums on the phone: David and Danielle as a family at Universal Studios, with David's son and her granddaughter; David and Danielle at expensive restaurants.

David was using his money to spoil Danielle. That's why he was always broke.

There were pictures of them all through his phone, just of him and her. David also had pictures of other women.

David was clearly a womanizer.

I was too naive and in love to recognize all the signs. David didn't give a fuck about me.

He was living a double life.

Hell, if Danielle truly knew who this man was, I highly doubt she would marry him.

Maybe that would be David's karma. Men couldn't take the same hurt they give women.

I picked up my phone. "Wait until I tell Monica this." She picked up on the second ring. "Monica. Are you busy?"

"No, I'm just doing laundry. What's going on?"

"I found David's old phone. This is the phone that broke a few months back. It wouldn't turn on before, but today, I tried it and it turned on perfectly."

"Did you find what you were looking for?"

"I did, and so much more."

"Is it the bad?" Monica questions.

"Yes, it is. I think Danielle should know exactly who she is marrying. She has no clue about who he is."

"Do you know when the wedding is?"

"Yes. It's June 29. That's in three weeks."

"Right!"

"Monica, David used me, I gave him everything. But I wasn't the only one Mo, nor is Danielle. He is seeing so many other women. It hurts Monica. This whole time, this is what he was doing. I can't let him get away with it. I'm going to the wedding and expose him. Danielle has no clue of the man she is marrying. David thinks he can just discard me like trash, fuck that!"

• • •

"Jayla, I don't think that's a good idea. You will just look like a crazy woman who is still in love."

"Not if I show up with the proof, Monica. He can't lie his way out of it."

"That's true, but if you show up and expose him, and she still marries him, then what, J?"

"Then, it's on her. But, fuck man, it felt like a knife is just ripping out my heart entirely. He used me, and then had the audacity to put all the blame on me. I didn't deserve that, Monica."

"No, you didn't, but David never deserved you, either. Let them get married in peace, that's her headache now. Don't lose who you are trying to prove a point. You have too much class to be acting like a fool. Yes, it hurts, it's going to hurt until it no longer does. I just want you to remember the woman you were before you met David. You had style and grace, you had confidence in yourself. Remember who you are."

"Monica, I can't remember that now. David, can't get away with it. After I expose him, I'll go back to having style and grace. But right now, I am just going to be raw and ruthless."

"Just think twice before you act, Jayla. Sometimes, the point we are trying to prove ends up costing us more than we think we gain."

"I hear you, Mo, but right now, I need to figure some things out."

"Be good to yourself. Just remember he ain't worth it. Call me before you get yourself in trouble."

Monica was right, but who wanted to hear the truth right now? I certainly didn't.

I hung up with Monica and called...

"Hello."

"Keisha. Are you down to crash a wedding in three weeks?"

"Hell yeah."

"I have David's old cell phone, and you won't believe the shit I found in it."

● ● ●

113

"J, I can believe it, without you even explaining it to me.
Are you okay?"

"I'm not! But I will be once we expose him. I'm not sure if I can ever trust men again. He even has a sex tape on his phone of him having unprotected sex with another woman."

"Was it with Danielle?"

"No, it was with another woman."

"He had women sending him pussy pictures and text messages. This shit made my stomach turn in knots just reading it."

"We can do whatever else you want to do, Jayla; I'm down. Shit, give me the info, and I'll make it my top priority to find out where the wedding is located and cancel every god damn thing. Everybody will be surprised; I'll cancel the venue, the DJ, the caterer, and whatever else. Give me their address and I'll have both of their cars towed before the wedding day. We can definitely even the score."

I laughed, unintentionally. "Keisha, girl, you are crazy. But, thanks for having my back."

"No problem, sis. I know it hurts. So, whatever we have to do to make you whole and happy again, that's what we will do. And then, we will deal with the consequences later."

"Thank you, Keisha."

"Call me, Jayla. Don't do anything without me."

"I won't, Keisha."

Right as I hang up with Keisha, I heard a knock on my door.

"Who is it?" I shouted out.

"It's Ricki. Now, open up."

"Ricki, what are you doing over here?"

"I was just in the neighborhood, and I wanted to stop and check on you.

I brought you a bottle."

"A bottle of what?"

"Jack N Daniels."

● ● ●

114

"I don't believe you were just in my neighborhood. What brings you over?"

"You are right. Monica called me to come check on you."

Ricki and I walked over to the kitchen table.

Ricki took out two red cups and a bottle of Jack Daniels and Coke.

"I heard what happened, J, and I feel for you. I really do. He is a fucked up dude. Let me first start by saying this, I don't care about what he didn't see you in, it's his loss. I want you to know, you are enough and deserve better. David did you the favor of saying goodbye. He didn't deserve you; I just wish you understand that. There's no prize by being his wife. He wasn't paying your rent, or your bills, or even bringing his check home to you. So, my question to you is, what are you losing?

"You had a whole grown man, living off you, not contributing to the rent or bills, and you were helping him with his bills. So, my question again, is what were you holding on to? A warm body in the bed, with a cold heart?

"Wait, let me guess... The dream he sold you in the beginning; you fell for his potential. You wanted to be his ride or die and stay down with him throughout the bullshit, just to prove you love him?"

I reached over, grabbed the Jack, and poured until my cup was half full.

I couldn't even give an answer; Ricki took the words right out of my mouth.

"Jayla, I'm just going to keep it one hundred with you and I mean no disrespect. You were just his dummy. He smelled weakness and he played on it. He took it as far as you allowed him, too. Hell, he didn't have to work for anything, you gave him everything without earning it. A man won't value a woman he didn't have to work for. I'm not saying you're easy. But shit, you gave him your house key after only a few months of knowing him. I'm sure he didn't do anything special, but just giving you a little attention.

"That's the game fuck boys play. I know, I used to be a fuck boy too until I grew up and became a man. I know the game, I tried to warn you early on, but you wouldn't listen; you were too far gone in love. After a while, I got tired of talking and listening to you complaining about it; you had to learn the hard way, I see.

"J, he never gave a fuck about you. It was obvious, maybe not to you, because you were blinded by what you thought was love or could have been love.

"But we all saw it, how your self-esteem dropped. Every time you came around, you would look sad or we could tell you just got done crying; you weren't the same anymore."

"You're right, I wasn't the same. I questioned myself about what I lacked as woman that made me unable to keep his attention solely on me. I thought maybe I wasn't good enough, wasn't woman enough, or was just not pretty or experienced enough for him. I dealt with a lot of disrespectful shit, even things I thought I would never tolerate until I started tolerating the bullshit. Toward the end of the situation, he would tell me, 'Ain't no man going to want you.' My self-esteem was shattered on the inside. I loved him and I couldn't figure out what was I lacking as woman. I couldn't hold my head down in front of him; it was only when I was out of his presence that I would cry.

"For a moment, I blamed my upbringing as tomboy, thinking maybe I lacked something growing up, maybe I wasn't on my grown woman status. I had to tell him that growing up, I was a tomboy, I had all brothers. But as I grew up into my adulthood, I changed and started wearing dresses, heels, and make up. I mean, before I met him, I never had a hard time getting a man's attention. In fact, most of them loved the fact that I loved sports or could play basketball. I was all woman in their eyes, I'm sure."

"J, fuck their eyes. Were you all woman in your own eyes? Those are the only pair of eyes that matter. What matter most is how you see yourself."

● ● ●

"I was all woman, to me. I knew I had to grow and develop in some areas, but I saw a woman while looking in the mirror."

"And that's all that mattered then," Ricki interrupted. "Don't allow anyone to come into your life and mistreat you, or have you questioning yourself of who you are. Hell, David was just putting his insecurities off of you. You got your shit together, your career, your own home, businesses, your own everything. Yet, what does he have? What has he accomplished? What can he bring to the table besides his insecurities, insults, and dick?

"I want you to remember this, when a man hates himself, he takes it out on the woman who loves him. He knew you loved him, but he didn't have any respect for you.

"And he didn't have too because you kept accepting his bullshits. So, why would he respect you? He already had you in the Weak Women's category that he could walk all over. What's standing behind door number 1 after he has been gone for several days and not responding to calls or text messages? Are you ready for this answer? Jayla, the door mat, and, who's going to accept him without questioning him? He tested you many times and you failed to set your boundaries or demand your respect. A strong woman would have had his shit outside and changed her locks.

"Men don't like weak women; we like women who set boundaries, a woman who won't allow us men walk all over them, a woman who takes no shit. I'm not calling you a weak woman, but what I saying is, grow some balls. Don't allow someone to treat you poorly just because you love them. Fuck him.

"I bet if you would have changed your locks and not given him the key back, he would have respected you. He would have had to earn it back. Now, at that point, he would have gone on about his way or he would have given you the respect you deserved and demanded. But you didn't. So, moving forward, never give a man a key to your place until his name is on the lease too and he is paying the whole rent or

●●●

mortgage. And if your next boyfriend or husband ever miss a night out, you better check his ass and have his shit packed that night. Set the tone that you are not putting up with bullshit. I promise you, he will call you even if he thinks he is going to be late for dinner. He doesn't want those problems.

"I'm going to put you up on game. You have to train a man how to treat you. We are like Dogs; you throw the Frisbee, we go get it and we get rewarded. And that's how you have to look at it from now on. You have the power, and never forget that. Never forget your worth and value. A man that's for you is coming to go out his way to be with you. You don't have to open up your legs or wallet. I mean, yeah we want what's between them, that's the goal, but that's not going to be the only reason we want you. Let the next man work for you.

"Speaking of opening up your wallet, look, I even get why you helped ole boy out. He was having hard times financially, and that was thoughtful of you. But, he took advantage of you. Did he ever pay you back? Wait, never mind. I already know the answer to that, too. No, he didn't. He didn't have to. What was the consequence if he didn't? You changing the locks? Putting him out? Not helping him again? He already had you figured out. He could blow his money and be broke knowing you would bail him out. How many times did he bail you out when you were short? I recall when your car got towed and he played the broke role. Yet, when his car got repossessed, you paid $1,284.45 to get his car back. Did he pay you back? Wait, I can answer that too because I know the game. No, he didn't. You were his life line, his dummy, his captain S-a-v-e A H-o-e.

"Not to throw it in your face, but I just want you to see the truth in case you're still blinded. Didn't you get his car out of the repossession days before Valentine? And, didn't he disappear on Valentine's Day and resurfaced days after? So, you do know that he was smashing another chick for Valentine.

"I know you were pissed the hell off; you could have kept your $1,284.45 in your pocket and treat yourself to something nice, instead of paying his bill. He didn't give a fuck. Like I said, he had you figured out. And once again, a strong woman should have recognized she was being used and cut herself off from him. And by no mean am I calling you weak, I'm just pointing out the games fuck boys play. You can't have a giving heart; you have to let man be man, and let them figure shit out on their own. It's not your responsibility to help anyone. Wait, so let me just put it out all on the table since we are on the topic of money. Did he ever pay you back the $600? You know, the money you gave to him to get his license back, or what about the $1500 you gave him to help pay his attorney for his child custody? Hmmm... I bet I can answer this, too. This man saw sucker written all over you. I want you to just stop giving people who tend to fall in love with your hand and not your heart."

"I know, I'm embarrassed. I did it all from my heart, helping him and he had the nerves to tell me anybody could have done that for him. Shit, I wish I had someone like me in my life when I was struggling and coming up short. I feel so foolish."

"Don't feel foolish. Take this as a learning experience; set your standards higher when it comes to men. Expect more from them. Date a man that's financially stable, who have his own, who don't mind helping you, at least, at the point you know he is not sticking around just to use you or benefit off you. Make sure the next man has ambition and more than one way to earn money. I'm not talking about illegal, but a hustle like cutting hair, lawn care, something he can go to when money is tight and he can make something happen. A man that's a provider; no more leeches. You are under no obligation to help anybody with anything. They can save themselves, and if they can't, that's on them.

"Danielle didn't get the prize because she got his last name, what she got was a man child. She may even have to provide for their family eventually, when he can't produce. When they were dating, he had the money to pay her bills or take her out because he had his whole check. Now that they live together, she may require him to pay bills. So now, where's the extra money he once had before to wine and dine with her?

"Or, he'll have excuses of, I'm working on a business and when I make it big, I'm going to take care of you. I'm sure she'll believe it for a while, the same way you believed it.

"But sooner or later, she'll get tired and finally see who she really married.

"Listen to me clearly, a Lion doesn't change its stripes.

"I can literally beak down every part of your experiences and tell where you went wrong for accepting the bullshit. But I know you feel enough hurt and betrayal. My only purpose is to show you it was over before it started and that you were the only one who kept giving life to a dead situation.

"It was nothing for David to walk away from you because he never invested in you in the first place, you were the only one investing in him with your emotions and everything else he could benefit from. I know it hurts, but just remember the hurt so you never make this mistake again. It's a cold world out here, filled with opportunists. I don't want this fucked situation to make you bitter become a mad, bitter woman. But instead, let it make you better. This time around, you are smarter and stronger in the selection process in dating. When they show you who they are this time around, believe them. A man will tell you everything you need to know, if you just listen.

"You're a good woman, and there are good men out there. Now, just love yourself, and I mean, really love yourself. If you need me, J. I'm here for you. I'm rooting for you. Most importantly, I love you and I want to see you happy again.

And you know, I'm always going to keep it real with you.

I want to share a quote with you by T.D. Jakes: 'There are people who can walk away from you, let them walk. I don't want you to try to talk another person into staying with you, loving you, calling you, caring about you, coming to see you, staying attached to you. Their destiny is never attached to you; your destiny is never tied to anybody that left. And it doesn't mean they are bad persons, it just means that their part in the story is over. And you got to know when people's part in your story is over.'

"Now, this time around, you know the game." Ricki reached over and gave me a hug. "You are one hell of a woman. Never ever allow a man to dim your light because of his own insecurities within himself. Be good to yourself; you worth it!"

CHAPTER 8
*Ain't this Some Sh***

"Hi. Can I help you?" This fine, brown-skinned, 6'4 athletic built man asked me, as he stood behind the counter at the Sprint store. I walked toward him.

"Yes. I'm here to pay my phone bill."

"I'm here to help you," he said, with a smile. What's your number?"

"515-555-5551."

"And the password to your account?"

"Kitten."

"You have a past due amount of $158.00. How much would you like to pay today?"

"What's the least I can pay to keep it on?"

"To be honest with you, since it's past due, you may want to pay the full balance. I would hate to see you get your services interrupted."

I took a deep sigh and exhaled. "I'll pay the full balance." I looked at his name badge, and it reads: Josh Jones.

Josh laughed. "I understand the feeling." We both laugh. "I grew up with my mom and she always paid the minimum to keep the bills on," Josh shared, jokingly.

I reached down in my black leather purse, looking for my debit card. "Here's my debit card. I'll pay the past due amount." I passed Josh my debit card across the counter.

"Do you play basketball?" Josh asked me, as he continued my transaction.

"I do, but how did you know?"

"I saw the basketball symbol on your class ring."

"Yes, I played in High school."

"You can ball!" He said surprisingly.

"I will ball your ass right on up," I replied confidently while looking Josh directly in the eyes. "You don't want any."

Josh smiled and handed me my receipt, debit card, and his business card. "Here's my number. Call me when you are ready for the challenge."

I took all three, turned around, and headed toward the door. There was nothing left to say. Josh had no idea of how bad I would embarrass him on the court. Once I stepped out of the Sprint store, I texted Josh as I made it to the car.

"I'm ready for the Challenge. Game on, homeboy. Lock me in! Now, the ball is in your court."

Josh responded back instantly. "I was hoping you would text me and take me up on my challenge, lol. This evening, I'm playing in a Basketball League at 4:30 p.m. in Gardena at the Rowley Gym. If you are free, come out and check me."

"I'll let you know, but if I do decide to go and I see you warming the bench or air balling, you owe me gas money for wasting my time and gas."

"Bet. I got you, beautiful."

It was 2:35 p.m. I had enough time to run a few errands and make it to his game.

✳✳✳✳✳✳✳

I walked into Rowley Gym in anticipation to see Josh on the court. I didn't have any expectations; most people talk about a good game, but I want to see if for myself.

The referee blew the whistle, foul on number 34. I continued to make my way to the bleachers, along with the others. I sat down in just enough time to watch the opposite team player shoot his two free throws. As I scan the court, I didn't see Josh. The next place I look was the team benches, and there goes Josh with a white sweatband around his forehead in a green jersey with the big "12" on the front with black basketball shorts and a pair of Jordan's on his feet. Josh just sat there with his elbows on his knees and knuckles under his chin as he watched everyone else play.

A whistle ble, the referee yelled, "Sub." Josh jumped up off the bench and ran onto the court as his other team member ran toward the bench. Josh got into the position of defense. His opponent was about six-six, weighing maybe about one hundred eighty. He was definitely taller than Josh and has a longer arm advantage.

But, if Josh had as much game as he claimed, he should be able to keep up.

After the game, Josh walked me to my car. "Thanks for coming, Jayla. I appreciate the support."

"No problem, Josh. I just enjoy watching others play basketball. Plus, I had to come to check you out and see if you really have skills like you said."

"So, what do you think?"

"You're all right. I mean, you ain't no Kobe and you definitely can't beat me, but you can play. I would pick you up on my squad if I ran a full-court game."

"Really?"

"Yeah, really," I joked.

Josh hugged me. "I'm about to head home and shower up. If you're free tonight, let's do dinner."

"I possibly could make myself available this evening for dinner." I smiled.

● ● ●

"Okay, cool. So, when you are ready, let me know. We can meet at Killer Shrimp in the Marina, or if you're comfortable, I can pick you up and we can go together."

"I'll drive myself.

"Okay. Well, just give me a time and I'll be there."

I look down at my watch, it's 6:15 pm. Let's meet by 8:30?"

"Sounds like a date. I'll be there."

✳✳✳✳✳✳✳

"Mo, I met a man. He is tall, dark, and handsome. I prayed the other night asking God to send me someone to distract me from my heartache from David. And *boom*, he appeared. He seems to be a gentleman. We went on a few dates and he makes me happy, and I haven't thought about David as much."

"That's great, Jayla. Just don't' rush into another relationship to get your mind off your past situation. That's exactly how you end up hurt again.

Be careful before you open your heart or get close to someone. Ask God to reveal his true character. God will, and when He does, don't make excuses. You're still vulnerable, and I don't want to see you getting hurt again."

"Yeah, I know, Mo. I am being cautious. I told Josh I was low-key crazy at this point. I told him, 'The next man that plays me, I'm going to tase him.' We are both going to end up shocked. I laughed the joke off with him. But, in all honesty, I was serious, not about tasing, however. I'm stuck between: I don't want to feel that type of hurt again, but I want to feel that type of love again."

"Just be careful, J."

"I am, Mo. I really am. He even offered to lower my cell phone bill after we left breakfast yesterday morning. He was going to apply some of his company's perks to my bill. He told me that he has a family plan with five lines, unlimited everything and he only pays $200 per month. I was like, 'Hook a sister up. He said he had me in. I even got the email confirmation that changes were made to my account this morning."

"So, did he put you on his account?"

"To be honest, I don't know, but I hope not, because then, he will have access to my calls and texts history, and I don't need him to be all in my business like that."

"I think you need to check, just to make sure, Jayla. I mean, I like the fact that he comes in trying to be helpful, but I also think you should just make sure."

You're right, I will. I love you, Mo. Thank you for always having my back through all this craziness in my life."

"I got you, J."

"Thank you. I'm going to head over to Sprint now and see what changes he made to my account."

"Hi. Welcome to Sprint."

I approached the front corner. "Hi. My name is Jayla Jones and I just want to get some information on my account."

"Sure, Ms. Jones. I will be happy to assist you. Let me get some information and I'll pull up your account. You've been verified, Ms. Jones. How can I assist you?"

"I was just coming in to see if there were any changes made to my account recently."

"Sure. Let me check that out right now."

"How many lines do you have on your account, Ms. Jones?"

"Just one."

"Well, I see here you have ten open lines."

"Excuse me?"

The Sprint sales representative turned the computer screen around. "See, here it is. There are nine new lines added to your account. Actually, these are very new numbers."

"I didn't authorize any new lines to my account."

"Wait, there's actually another phone being added to your account right now. I'm going to print out all the sales receipts. If you didn't authorize this, then we must contact the Fraud Department immediately. I'll be back in a moment; I need to get the receipts from the back printer."

"What the fuck?" I say to myself. "I can't deal."

Martha, the sales representative, came back with ten invoices. I looked through each of them in disbelief. I was played for a fool again. I pulled out my cell phone and called Monica.

"Mo, you won't believe what I just found out. Mo! I got fucked over again."

"Wait. What?"

"This muthafucka who works at Sprint added nine lines to my account. Each line, he added an iPhone Imax."

"What! How the hell did he do that?"

"I don't fucking know. I'm at Sprint now. The cashier is printing me all the receipts. His name is on all the receipts as the cashier for all the equipment. He put all the phones on a lease to pay plan. He even changed the email on my account to his so I wouldn't get the emailed receipts. What a fucking crook."

The Sprint sales representative handed me all the receipts for each transaction made. As I went through each one, I shook my head in disbelief. *How the fuck did I allow someone to fuck me over again?*

Nine iPhones, two iWatches, two pairs of EarPods, and a Sprint drive. This muthafucka charged over $10,000 of equipment on my account in over two days.

Before I could get it all out, Monica walked through the Sprint doors.

● ● ●

"I was still across the street, getting something to eat when you called," Monica said.

I handed over all the receipts to Monica; she looked through them for a second time.

"This shit doesn't make any sense," Mo said.

"I know, right?"

"We can start the fraud claim right now," said Martha. "I'm sorry to say, but he just added a new line to your account. Here's your new transaction receipt." Martha promptly picked up the phone and called the Fraud Department. "Hi, I'm Martha from Sprint Store #654. I have a customer in front of me who has been a victim of fraudulent activity on her account. Even while she is in the store with me, two new lines have been added. She also stated that she didn't give anyone authorization to add new services to her account..."

Martha continued to talk to the Fraud Department, while Monica and I spoke to each other.

"Jayla, you're too open. Close your heart to love for a moment. Right now is not the time. You're still hurting. The universe is going to give the exact same lesson in different versions over again until you master it. This is one of the most single important laws you can learn about the nature of reality. Everything else builds upon this."

Monica knew me well enough. She knew was I trying to fill a void and patch up the pain. She gave me the hug I needed at that time.

"Focus on your goals, Jayla," she whispered into my ear. "Love the shit out of yourself. You don't need anyone else to help you heal."

"Ms. Jones," Martha said. "The Fraud Department gave me a case number for you and a list of instructions. We are going to remove all the charges off your account, however, you need to go file a police report and bring us a copy, and we will send it over to the Fraud Department. I do apologize for this incident. If you have any more questions or concerns, please don't hesitate to contact me directly. Also, for the time being, we have to block your account so Josh Jones won't have access to it. The Fraud Department is opening up an investigation and will handle matters accordingly. Once again, I am sorry for this occurrence."

Josh was a dead man walking. Between him and David, I was over men and their charming lies. I told Josh that I wasn't to be played with, and yet, he did this bullshit. I'm done.

For the next few days, I ignored all of Josh's phone calls and text messages. There was nothing to talk about. I was completely done with him; he thought he could get away with it.

Josh's text messages became more frequent as days passed on.

"Hey. Are you okay?"

"I miss you."

"I called, you didn't answer."

"I won't bother you anymore."

"I see you are not talking to me, but I want to let you know I am in the hospital."

"Hi."

"Hello."

To be honest, I didn't care if he wass in the hospital or not. I wasn't going to respond to that. All of it was manipulation to get me to respond.

"Hi, how are you?"

"Is there anything you want to tell me?" I finally texted him back.

"As far as when? You've been ignoring me. Just ask me."

"Should I trust you?"

"I'm about to call you, and yes, I hope; that's all I want."

"Is this your email address? flyball09**@gmail.com?

"Yes, it is."

"I placed that on your account temporarily to get your discount, and I was contacting you to switch it back, but no reply."

"Anything else you want to tell me?"

• • •

"Yep, I will call and tell you if you answer."

"I'm sure I won't answer. So, I'm going to ask you one last time, is there anything else you want to tell me?"

"You won't answer my call, but yes, there is something I want to tell you. Am I right?"

"No, I won't answer! Because I trusted you. I told you the last man fucked me over and you told me you were different. You even told me to take a chance on you and you fucked me over, too!"

"I am already fixing your account. So, I did some things to give you a discount and to check to see how you would like it, but I will set everything back to normal."

"Josh, don't ever speak to me again. It's too late."

"I told you I would never mess with you. I'll fix it."

"You know exactly what you did to my account. Nothing was authorized in any way. That was completely dishonest and untrustworthy. You ain't different; you are just like every other muthafucka, and for a moment, I thought I found a gentleman, someone I could let my guard down with, someone who could be honest with me. I was fucking wrong."

"You did. I really like you. I was trying to help. I checked some things and I didn't do anything to mess it up. I put that on my daughter, you are wrong. I really want you in my life and I'm willing to prove it."

"So tell me, what did you add to my account?"

"I need your password so I can put everything back to normal."

"Why did you do that to me? Out of all the people you know, why me? You said you weren't trying to fuck me over, but you did! You are still not telling me everything."

"I'm going to tell you, but first, can I get your password?"

"Hell, no! The same way you did it is the same way you need to fix the shit."

"You are looking at this in the wrong way. Can you please tell me your password?"

● ● ●

"I'm looking at it wrong, huh? Yet, you did everything."

"No, I asked you if I can I explain by talking to you, but you won't allow me. Let me prove you wrong."

"Prove me wrong then."

"It won't let me change anything without your password. How can I prove you wrong? I can't fix it."

"That's not a problem. You need to figure it out. It's above me now."

"Okay, I'm trying."

"So, since you don't want to come right out and tell me. Where are the ten lines of equipment? The iPhones, two iWatches, and two EarPods? That totaled over $10,000 worth of equipment I didn't authorize!"

"Wait, that isn't accurate, but it has been fixed. And if you don't want to talk, then I can't make you. I'm sorry you think that someone is out to get you, but that's not true. It was an error made. It got messed up, but wasn't finalized. We had an issue with the system, but it's on me."

"I like you, I really did. We had a lot in common. I even let down my guards and tried to trust again. You asked me to take a risk, whether we are going to make it or not, and I decided to be all in. I can't be so naive to believe this was an error when certain things don't add up. At a certain age, things aren't misunderstandings or mistakes to me anymore. But one thing I did learn is, a muthafucka will try to get over on you! And if you don't catch it, they will play the role like nothing happened. Fuck, here I go again disappointed – the very thing I didn't want to be. Fuck this love shit. Dudes ain't loyal to anyone, but themselves."

"Listen, I told you. I know how it feels to be hurt and loyal. I made a mistake. I wasn't trying to hurt you or mess you up. I promise it was just a mistake that happened. I was just trying to play with the numbers to see what I can do for you. I am asking, please don't give up on me. Please, give me a second chance and let me prove to you

● ● ●

that I am real, because I do believe that you are what I need in my life. Please, give me another chance."

"Josh, a mistake happens once, with one charge, one time. But it was nine charges over two days at different times. That's nine mistakes with different equipment. Is that really a mistake? Because that look intentional."

"Not intentional, I promise. Can you please not give up on me or walk away?"

"Then, what the fuck was it then?"

"I was just trying to see how I can benefit you and make you have a discount with my numbers, and surprise you with some things. But I fucked up, okay. I messed up no matter what I was trying or wanted to do. It was wrong and I made you uncomfortable, and I'm sorry."

"Fuck you and your 'I'm sorry.' That doesn't mean shit to me. I actually trusted you. I was even excited about what was to come. I told you the last dude played me and how heartbroken I was left. What the fuck were you thinking? An easy come up? Fuck you!"

"Who got an easy come up? Not me. But I see you don't want me, so I won't contact you again."

"Peace out!" I respond. "Block and delete."

✳✳✳✳✳✳✳

Hell, I was not about to put myself in the exact same situation again and not take heed. David taught me a thing or two when it came to cussing. Anybody could be called a muthafucka or get a 'Fuck you,' as we gained confidence in ourselves; red flags were no longer red flags, they were deal-breakers.

I was taking a break from dating. I just needed to heal.
I did it again; I let the wrong one in.
This time, the man stole from me.
I must have had 'USE ME' written all over me.

I isolated myself from everyone, turned off my cell, closed my blinds, and lay in bed. I was depressed and mad at myself; I was just through.

CHAPTER 9
A Word

I turned on the radio. I needed to get out of my head and place my thoughts elsewhere. I scanned through the radio stations.

"Come down to The Church of Deliverances," I heard in a deep, powerful voice. "I don't know who I'm talking to, but God put this in my spirit to tell you to come down and be delivered. Service starts by 7:00 p.m. Come as you are, come and be delivered. Just come as you are, leave the hurt, pain, and depression at the altar. God is a healer; you just have to open your heart to God and say yes. Come on down. Yes, I'm talking to you. I declare a breakthrough in your life. Once again, service starts by 7:00 p.m. I'm looking forward to your deliverance."

"Look at me, I can't go to church looking like this. I have on a pair of grey workout pants, a white t-shirt, and black sandals. I look in my rearview mirror, and my eyes were puffy and red. I've cried so much that I hid behind black shades. But, I can't wear these shades into the church. I remind myself, literally, if I were going, it would be as I am. I take a deep sigh and consider just going the next Sunday. I'll be properly dressed, and hopefully, I won't be needing to hide the behind the dark shades…"

The pastor's voice interrupted my rambling.

"Don't let the devil talk you out of your deliverance, don't let that phone call distract you, don't let self-doubt keep you from your deliverance tonight, come as you are. Walk into your deliverance with a smile on your face, let the Holy Spirit erase every frown. Walk into your deliverance, the doors will be open; you just have to walk through them. Somebody needs to hear this: 'Them wounding you was your freedom to walk away."

"Okay," I said aloud. "I'm going." I looked at my watch; service was to start in thirty minutes. I turned the radio off.

"Lord, can I be honest with you for a moment? My spirit is troubled, my mind is scattered, and my heart is broken. I am angry and there's a lot of regret in my heart. I'm seeking peace and I'm searching for it all in the wrong places. I sought love, but I didn't love myself. Lord, order my footsteps, lead me in the way I should go, strengthen my walk and relationship with you, build my confidence; I need you. I don't even know how it's all going to work out, nor do I know how it's all going to come together or how You will put it all together. But, I need you, I need you to take the wheel of my life before I get myself in trouble. God, I need you now. The feelings of hurt, shame, defeat, and betrayal are consuming me. Help me not be disappointed when a chapter closes, but rejoice that better days are ahead. Fix my heart, Lord. I speak healing and wholeness over my life. I trust God, I trust you."

I exited off the 405 Freeway, Manchester exit.

I walked into the church and a beautiful woman wearing a white dress greeted me. "Welcome to The Church of Deliverance. Have you been here before?"

"No, this is my first time here."

"Praise the Lord. "You are in for a deliverance tonight.

My name is Sister Patty.

"Hi, Sister Patty. My name is Jayla."

She leaned in and gave me a hug. "We are so glad you are able to join us this evening. Please follow me, I'll show you where to sit."

● ● ●

136

I followed Sister Patty to the front of the church. She sat me in the second row from the altar. I was the only one in that row. As I sat down; other church members greeted me with hugs, brief introductions, and smiles.

"Nice to have you. I'm Sister Joyce."

"Hi, I'm Jayla."

"We are so happy to have you this evening. God bless you, my dear. You are in for a blessing this evening. I promise you will not leave the same way you came in. Just leave whatever you're battling with at the altar tonight."

I smiled, trying to hide the fact that hours earlier I was crying, plotting, hurt, and angry.

Moments later, the church began to fill. I was no longer the only one on that row. There was a woman wearing blue jeans and a sweater to my left side, and an older woman to my right wearing a long yellow dress.

I focused my attention on the altar and watched the pastor walk to the pulpit. The pastor introduced himself as Pastor Nelson and began to talk to the whole congregation.

"It's so good to see everyone one more time in the house of the Lord," he said as he opened his Bible. "I'm going to start the service. Please, hold the hand of the person next to you and close your eyes as I lead us in prayer.

"Dear Heavenly Father,

We thank you, we thank you for allowing us to come together in Your house one more time to praise your Name. Lord, use me as Your vessel to deliver your word and only your word. God, I ask You to heal and restore every hurting heart, stressed-out mind, broken-down body, and out-of-control life in the building tonight. Father, we ask for Your assistance in letting go of ideas, old patterns, or habits that no longer serve us. We are praying against the spirit of blockage and barriers. We ask You to break every barrier that blocks us from being close to You. I rebuke every spirit of depression, addiction, heartbreak, loneliness, and suicide. I ask you to heal those who are hurting on the inside and going through things they don't speak of. Bring them peace. Father God, we lift up all those who are facing illness today, we ask that You would bring healing and comforting peace to their bodies and minds. Calm their hearts and let them experience the healing power of Your love. I also pray for those who need direction, remind us, Lord, that you have a plan, all we have to do is just call on You and wait for You. God, let your word be a lamp and light to our paths. I pray to God that You touch every single one of us this evening and meet our needs. I pray an end to every battle that's draining you emotionally, spiritually, mentally, physically, and financially in Jesus' Name, Amen.

"...I don't know who this message is for tonight, but know that God is restoring your strength! You're being renewed and refreshed for better days. Everything lost will be repaid. Open up your Bible to Joel 2:25. Read with me. God can restore what is broken and change it into something amazing, all you need is faith. Faith," Pastor Nelson repeats with conviction. "You may be dealing with a sickness, a loss, a bad break up, maybe you even feel life has dropped you, but you need to get ready, God is about to pick you back up. He will not just bring you out the same, but He will bring you out better than before. No matter what you are facing, remember the Lord is right there with you. Turn to Deuteronomy 20:4: 'The Lord, your GOD is the one who goes with you to fight for you against your enemies to give you victory.' God is saying, 'I will never send you into a situation alone; I go before you, I walk behind you. Whatever situation you are facing right now, be confident that I am with you.'

"I'm going to do something different tonight. I'm going to pass each of you a square white paper. I want you to put down in it whatever you need deliverance from, I want you to leave it at the altar. And after you leave there, I want you to stand around this glass table here. I'm going to pray for each of you and bless you with the holy oil."

● ● ●

The ushers began to pass out white pieces of paper.

"On this paper, pour out your needs. Tonight is your deliverance. Once you're done, fold your paper in fours and leave it. Leave that burden at the altar, leave that disappointment at the altar, leave that heartbreak and betrayal at the altar, leave the spirit of depression, defeat, and addiction at the altar. Leave it at the altar."

I stood up and made my way to the altar with tears in my eyes. I follow the older woman sitting next to my right. She grabbed my hand. "Come on, honey. You're not by yourself. Leave whatever battles you at the altar. God told me to hold on to you tight as you stand before the altar."

I left my folded piece of paper on the glass table in front of the altar, along with the others. We remained standing around the glass table. The pastor went down the line, praying and blessing each of us. When the pastor reached me, he looked at my eyes and wiped his forehead with his white handkerchief.

"I have a word for you tonight. God is speaking to my spirit this very moment. God wants you to know that you are exactly where you're meant to be. Just as a child has to pass through a tiny channel on its way from the womb into life, so are you on your way to God. The biggest struggles in life will turn out to be some of your biggest blessings. Just hold on.

"I see the pain in your eyes, you've been hurting for some time. But God said you are being delivered from the depression; all I hear in my spirit is restoration, restoration. God is going to restore whatever didn't work. The Devil has tried to make you lose your mind many times. You've been betrayed in many ways; yet, you stood in the midst of your storm. You are still here because God is with you. He said, 'Fear not, I will not allow any weapon that is formed against you to prosper. I am going to turn things around and bless you in the presence of your enemies.' Just keep praying, holding on to your faith. Just know that the Devil is a liar. Satan knows you live in your feelings, that's why he'll try to meet you in them. But, no weapon of depression, brokenness, heartbreak, and confusion will stop you from growing into your purpose. This ugly part of your story you're living through right now is going to be one of the most powerful parts of your testimony.

"You are walking into a new season in your life. God is protecting you. I know you've invested a lot and the return has been low. I hear the Spirit says, 'The wait is over; you're coming into your season.' That man who left you recently and broke your heart, God said, 'Look at that betrayal as a blessing.' The last sign before a major breakthrough is betrayal. That's when God removes and exposes their true colors. If they are for you, they will stick around, but if they are not for you, the anointing will remove them. Just sit tight, God will give you back better than what you thought you lost. Just know it was their loss and not yours. Just because someone walked out of your life doesn't mean you aren't valuable. It just means they couldn't see it or appreciate it. God has better for you; they were not meant for you.

I see a little boy next to you. There's a baby near you…"

"I don't have any kids," I said into his microphone.

"I had a miscarriage a year ago."

He shook his head.

"I pray healing over your soul. Let all the rejection, hurt, brokenness, and anger be washed away by his words. God heard your prayers, just stay patient. God is going to bless you with another baby. Your first living child will be a boy, and your second will be a girl. Not just that, but God said, 'That husband you been praying for, he is on the way. He is going to show you what true love is. You're going to be telling a different story soon. One of healing, success, health, prosperity, love, happiness, peace, and joy. You're going to be stronger, wiser, and full of life."

I lifted my hands and started praising God, thanking Him in advance.

"Just speak it, declare this word over your life," the pastor said.

● ● ●

140

Echoes of "Amen" filled the church right along with "Yes, Lord. Yes, Lord."

"Your next chapter will be amazing. God is changing your storyline to happy, blessed, and healed. God is the author of this chapter, give God your weakness and he'll give you His strength. Whatever God promised will surely come to pass. It's yours, just walk into your season. You weren't rejected by this man. You were released! They didn't leave your life, I moved them, God said."

"Hallelujah, Hallelujah," I shouted.

I break out in a spirit of deliverance while rejoicing. "Yes, Lord. Yes, Lord. I can't do this on my own. I surrender all. I surrender this situation to You. Heal me, Lord!" I cried out.

"Show me how to take who I am to who I want to be and use it for a purpose greater than myself."

"Hallelujah. Yes, Lord." The Church of Deliverance erupted in praise and worship.

The choir began to sing "Deliver Me (This is My Exodus)" by Donald Lawrence and The Tri-City Singers, featuring Le Andria Johnson.

Church music hit different when you're being delivered.

"Lord, please don't let me go back to anything I had to pray my way out of."

CHAPTER 10
We Crashing It?

"Okay, J, it's the wedding day. What are we going to do? Are we crashing the wedding or are you going to let it go?"

I took in a long, deep, dramatic breath. "Keisha, I'm just going to let it go, he was never meant for me."

"My girl," Keisha said. "You made the right decision. Listen, we are picking you up in an hour. So start getting ready. We have a whole day planned for you. Put on your all-white maxi dress and gold sandals, it's all celebration today."

"A celebration of what?"

"A celebration of a new chapter in your life. Whether you realize it or not, a new woman was birthed in you, it was watered with pain, betrayal, and no self-love, but that only grew into you. Those were only seeds; now, here's the beautiful part, it will turn into strength, courage, and wisdom, and let's not forget the most important part, which is self-love."

"Thank you, Keisha."

"So, get ready and we will be on our way."

I hung up the phone.

"What was I ever tripping on in the first place?" I say to myself. I look in the mirror and cry my very last tear. I am not crying because David is marrying Danielle today. I am crying because, for the first time in three years, I realize I no longer have to worry about if David was coming home tonight if he was sleeping with another woman, or if I have to walk on eggshells because he had a bad day. No more blunt disrespect because I didn't answer the question straightforwardly. No more silent treatment. No more of me trying to prove myself to a man that never loved me. Keisha was right. Today is a day of celebration. I vow to never allow anyone to come into my life and abuse or use me again. From this day forward, I promise to love myself unconditionally more than anyone else. I come first. I vow to always let my voice be heard and stand up for myself no matter how uncomfortable it is. My voice won't be silenced. I snap my fingers with an attitude, while still looking in the mirror. I am an amazing woman. Damn it, I am all of that and a bag of chips. I vow to always walk in confidence and never beg for someone to either be in my life or stay in my life. Today, I accept the good in goodbye. This shit broke my heart, but it did open up my eyes. I'm not the first, neither will I be the last woman to experience losing herself to a man, staying longer than she should have, or even accepting the disrespect and taking him back time and time again after he had shown who he was. I was just a fool in love, but never again." I repeatedly said to myself, "Never again." I stared at my reflection in the mirror. "I forgive you. Jayla," I said to myself.

I walked away from the mirror and started to get ready to enjoy my celebration.

Thirty minutes later, my cell phone rings…

"Jayla, we are here," Monica said.

"Okay, here I come."

I grabbed my keys and walked out of the door.

All my girls greeted me happily.

It was Monica, Ashton, Keisha, and Denise, and they all have white dresses on, too.

"Get it, J. Let's go."

I opened the passenger's door and sat in the front seat.

● ● ●

"You look beautiful, Jayla. I hope you are ready. We planned something very special for you. You know we couldn't let you go through this day alone," Ashton said, sitting in the back seat directly behind.

"Thank you, ladies. I really appreciate y'all for having my back! I swear, y'all the best."

"Yeah, we know," Keisha joked. "Girl, we love you, and we just want to see you through this mess! Plus, we still need to keep our eye on you in case you have second thoughts."

"Y'all funny." I laughed.

"Jayla, are you not missing one thing?" Ashton asked.

"What's that?"

Ashton placed what felt like a hat on my braids. "Look in the mirror, Jayla."

I pulled down the sun visor and look in the mirror, and it was a golden crown with purple trimming.

"You were missing your crown queen. It fell off while you were chasing after that man. Welcome back, queen. We've missed you. And, you know, every queen with a crown named Jayla needs a karaoke mic, so here's your mic."

Ashton hands over to me a blinged-out, rose gold mic with four speakers on the side. My girls know me well.

I smiled from ear to ear. "I am so thankful that I have y'all in my life." I started to cry.

"Girl, we've got you," Denise says. "That's what sisterhood is all about."

"We all go through things at different times in our life, but when you have friends that truly love you, you will never go through it alone. And, we love you, J."

"I love y'all, too! I swear, I do."

Monica injects, "We are going to Santa Barabara, J. I know that's one of your favorite relaxation spots. It's a beautiful Saturday and the weather is perfect. We are going to spend the day off on a yacht, wine tasting, and mingling with others."

"Let's do this!" I say, happily. I turned on the radio and adjusted my crown.

♪♪♪

Why men great 'til they gotta be great?

♪♪♪

"Woo! That's Lizzo. Her new song, "Truth Hurts," Ashton said. "Turn it up! This song bangs!!! Ladies, if you know the words, rap along with me. J, bust out your mic!"

● ● ●

CHAPTER 11
Oh, Hell No

"You will never believe who called me today."

"Who?"

"David!"

"What! What the hell did he want? What possibly could there be to talk about?"

"I didn't even know. There is nothing left to say. He married Danielle. He probably just wanted to piss me off or use me for something. He even left a voicemail saying I should give him a call."

"Girl, he is a narcissist. He better go call his wife," Keisha said. "Yet, what's Danielle's number? Since he called us, I think it's about time we also have a 'Hello, may I speak to Barbara?' conversation. I think it's time for her to learn the truth. Sometimes, you have to show a muthafucka that you can be a muthafucka, too. Don't you?"

"You're right, I think so, too. Her number is 951-902—" I stopped midway through and chuckle. "I am still hurting emotionally and it is taking everything in me not to pop the fuck off. It's funny how you get older and experience life. Those old school classic songs we once sang as innocent kids who were yet to experience heartbreak and betrayal hit an arrow straight to the heart now. I understand the pains and emotions behind them. I remember when I was ten years old, my mother took me to the movies and we saw *Waiting to Exhale*. I didn't quite understand then why so many women were cheering on Bernadine as she set her cheating husband's car on fire in their front yard. I thought she was crazy.

But as a grown-up woman now, I understand completely. Let that shit burn; hell, pass me some matches and I'll set that shit on fire myself. When you invest your heart, time, body, and energy into someone for the sake of love, and they betray you, something inside of you snaps and dies, and you're never the same again. Hell, I wasn't always like this; my attitude came from hurt and betrayal and being way too forgiving and naive. But, that's my fault; David didn't lie about who he was, and he showed me on multiple occasions that he was a cheater, liar, asshole, and user. It was me; I lied to myself about who I thought he could be. I was naive to think that he could be a better man. I even convinced myself that I was the problem because I didn't know how to love him. Well, that was according to him. Hell, it might be the truth because it was obvious that I didn't even know how to love myself, and it clearly showed.

"All I know is David better leaves me the hell alone. He just doesn't know how close I was to setting his shit on fire," I said, as I picked up the lighter across from me on the table.

"Fuck him, Jayla. You've come too far," Keisha says, as she puts her pre-rolled blunt in her mouth and lights the tip with a blue lighter. "Don't let him occupy any space in your life or mind. You are in a zone, stay in that zone," Keisha says after taking a deep inhalation of her joint. You are no longer running after all his little whimsical actions. He thinks he can call or text, and you will answer. He just wants to see if you are still his puppet master. You're not that puppet for him anymore; his wife is. Just be thankful you got out, she is the one stuck with him now. She is not a better woman than you, she is just a new clay for him to shape into what he wants until he is tired of her and moves on. If anything, feel sorry for her because now, she is the one playing his game. This is your time to be happy again. I hope that you become filled with so much happiness that it heals every part of you.

"I love you, girl, and I want you to remain strong. Don't ever go back to what tried to break or use you. Always remember how he left and let that strengthen why you can never, ever go back. You may even find yourself missing him, but then, remember the disrespect..." Keisha pauses and starts to cough.

"You have to know your worth even if it gets lonely sometimes, J."

"You're right, you're right." I nodded, acknowledging that it was best to be alone than next to someone who gives zero fuck about you. "I held on to David because I did truly love him, or at least, thought of him. In the beginning, it was beautiful and I loved every moment of it. We were happy, he respected me, and we spent all our days and nights with each other. There was no lies and secrets, we exchanged the "I love you" frequently. I was in lust and confused it all for love, and when shit went south, I started to chase that high of "us." In the very beginning, I felt like an addict and loving David was my drug. So, I overlooked, forgave, and became blind. I wanted the "us" as we were in the beginning, and in the end, it almost destroyed me. Looking back, I was naive. We could never go back to the beginning, the damage has been done, the trust was broken, and the respect was thrown out of the window.

"The few times I was finally fed up and ready for him to leave, he would always say, 'You're just going to leave me like the rest of them. You are not different.' I was so focused on being different than the past women he dealt with that I couldn't see that I was being manipulated. But now, I see clearly, he is just an opportunist, a womanizer, and a user.

"I never would have thought it would end like this. But hell; who the hell am I kidding?

"I have to stop thinking, "No, they wouldn't do me like this", because, in reality, any muthafucka would do you exactly like that, as David did.

"I sold myself short. I'll never again make excuses for anyone's bad behavior. David taught me this lesson, thoroughly."

Keisha passed me the blunt. "Damn, J, you're not alone. There are too many women building dudes up for the next woman, while he's damaging them for the next man. They moved on with their life and they can give zero fuck about them or their feelings. And that's why when they show you who they are; you have to believe them the first time, it will save so much heartache later on."

"I agree. I will only play the fool once, and that was it."

"Some people are just M & M's," Keisha injects.

"M & M's?" I question.

"Yes, girl, Memories and Mistakes."

We both chuckled as the aroma of cannabis filled the room.

"He wasn't looking for a wife; he was looking for a caretaker. Count it all joy, girlfriend. God allowed him to marry someone else before you were bamboozled into marrying him. You should be glad the other woman took out the trash so you didn't have to. Now, she is walking in your shoes; Lions don't change their stripes. He will do the same to her if she ignores the signs, too. Hell, while he was planning a wedding with her, he was sleeping with you and others. Technically, their marriage was built on deceit and lies already. Like Monica said, you can literally fill in the blank with ANYTHING and it will always be better than him. It's so important that we learn what role we play in people's lives just so we don't have to overplay our part. Keep on healing, and you're doing it well."

"You're right! I am doing well. Therapy has been helping me a lot. I've been going at least once a week for the last few months.

The therapist helped me realize that I was dealing with a narcissist. To be honest, I never knew what a narcissist was or how to protect myself from one. She recommended that I read up on narcissism, and when I finally did, I broke down! If only I would have known then what I know now, I would have made better decisions. David had every sign of a narc., the pattern of a self-centered, arrogant-thinking, lack-of-empathy-and-consideration for others, manipulative, selfish, patronizing, and demanding person. And the list still goes on and on; I just didn't know.

"My therapist, Mrs. Smith, explained a relationship with a narcissist to me.

"You will go from being the perfect love of their life to nothing you do is ever good enough. You will give everything and they will take it all and give you less in return. Eventually, you will end up depleted emotionally, spiritually, and mentally, and probably get blamed for it all. But before they discard you, they have to line up their next victim. They will continue to confuse and string you along while setting up two illusions, one to make you think it's your fault and the second to show the new victim how desired they are. They anticipate that when they completely discard you, you will start calling, stalking, and freaking out so they can show the new victim how crazy in love you are. They will also anticipant that you'll contact the new victim, and thwart your plan for this also. It's a setup. The narcissist walks away from the destruction they've caused, looking like the good guy or even the victim. They are sneaky and live their lives fooling people. It's nothing, but a game and rotating players for them.

"She described the exact "Relationship" I had with David, I couldn't believe it. And that synopsis happened on my first visit with her."

✳✳✳✳✳✳✳

Before David called me, I was fine, having a wonderful day. But while watching his name appear across my phone, I could feel the shift in my emotions, I developed anxiety. It's been months since I've heard from David. Apart from wanting to answer the phone and ask him a million questions, then curse him out, the other part of me said, "Don't, just let it go."

I called my therapist immediately after David called.

"Hi, Mrs. Smith. I'm sorry to call you unexpectedly. David just called me."

"Did you answer?"

"No, I didn't. But I can feel my anxiety going up."

"Give yourself time to grieve the person you've lost, the friend, the partner, the love you thought you had. Give yourself the time you need to let him die and become a memory, instead of a trigger. Sometimes, we have to grieve people that are still alive. I want you to write David a farewell letter, get everything you have to say to him out. You don't have to mail it to him, you can burn afterward, bury it, do whatever with it, just don't keep holding on to it. So did you write the letter, Jayla?"

"I did. You want to hear it?"

****

David,

I stayed with you for so long throughout the bullshit because I was torn between not giving up on the person that I loved and coming to terms with the fact that the person I loved no longer existed inside the body that I was staring at and laying next to every night. That was a really difficult and painful thing to wrap my brain around, and it took a while to believe. I did not unlove you overnight, I unloved you in bits of pieces over time. I grew a new skin that you could never touch, a new heart that you could never break again, and a new soul that you could never corrupt. This is how I unloved

• • •

you, slowly, painfully, and the only thing is that I should have unloved you sooner.

As I was fighting for you, I realized I was fighting to be lied to, fighting to be taken for granted, fighting to be disappointed, fighting to be hurt again. So, I stopped fighting for you and started fighting to let go. And, to be honest, that was painful; my mind needed more time to accept what my heart already knew, that you weren't meant to be in my life forever, and your purpose was just to teach me a lesson, that I was to truly love and value myself. You always told me, "The closest one to you will hurt you the most." But I never wanted that person to be you and I never wanted to hurt you, either. I wanted to grow with you, build a life with you, and grow old with you. Looking back, we were two broken souls that needed healing in our lives. I couldn't see it then, but after us going our separate ways, I see everything clearly. I didn't know how to give you the love you are asking for, I just offered you everything that I had as a substitute. I opened up myself completely to you, and it wasn't enough for you to feel loved. But, it still didn't give you the right to disrespect me, use me, and take advantage of me.

Whatever love I gave you, it was the only love I knew how to give. I was genuine when it came to you. I wanted to be your student and learn your depths. I wish I could have met you before your heart turned cold, maybe we could have something more meaningful and less painful that manifested. I could see the cracks in you, you were damaged long before I met you. I get it now, especially after being damaged, too. The way you treated me had nothing to do with me, but everything to do with the issues within you. And how I allowed you to treat me had nothing to with you, but everything to do with how I felt about myself.

I can't blame everything on you. I wish I was strong enough, in the beginning, to confront you about Raquel being pregnant, instead of keeping it a secret when I knew. I can't lie, it was hard as hell knowing and not saying anything. But I didn't want to lose you nor was I ready to walk away,

● ● ●

even though the trust was broken from the very beginning. And because the trust was broken in the beginning, I put my guard up and started digging for the truth, which turned me into an investigator from then on.

It was hard for me to pay attention to your needs completely because I was distracted by my intuition telling me something wasn't right. Yet, while living with me, you blamed me for your inconsistencies, had me questioned myself wondering about what I lacked that had you continuously when fucking around with other women. But after long nights of doubting myself, I finally got my answer: This was your pattern, you cheated on every woman you dealt with, and I'm sure in time, Danielle will be no different. I was just crazy enough to think that I was different or that my love could change your behavior. I was only fooling myself. You were going to do what the fuck you've wanted to do anyway.

I can never understand which is more painful, the lies I believed or the truth I did not. I was living in a fantasy, and I thought we could fix the cracks in our relationship, and one day, we would be solid. But it was obvious that I was the only one trying to fix anything. You were already mentally and emotionally invested somewhere else. It's funny because after the weekends you disappeared and come back, the first thing you did was lay in my bed and fucked me.

I get it, you only did what I allowed. I didn't have any boundaries, and you knew I would allow it. You never came back because you loved me or wanted to make things work, you came back because it was convenient for you. You had a free roof over your head, you didn't have any pay bills, you had hot meals without buying groceries, and got a pussy with a bit of head on the side. And in return, I didn't require you to do anything. We both knew that wasn't healthy; yet, what I allowed continued. I can't put the blame on you entirely, I played my part. I can't even expect any apology from you because you really don't give a fuck. The only one that owes me an apology is myself. I put up with a lot of shit I didn't deserve. I was the only one hurting myself when it came down to it. It was my responsibility to get up from the table when respect was no longer being served.

Instead, I remained seated down and loyal.

I was too fucking loyal. To be completely honest, I never stepped out and fucked anyone else while we were in our situation. You had my full attention. Although other men tried to get my attention, I only had eyes for you. Looking back, I could have missed the opportunity to meet my husband due to my focus on you, because surely, you found your wife.

What an experience! You were the first man I allowed to live with me. I'll never play house again nor will I be captain S-A-V-E A H-O-E. I can't save anybody. I'll never put myself in a position to be suckered or go broke again trying to help someone. You see, when I was helping you, I was struggling, too. I didn't really ask you for help because you didn't always have it, according to you. And the times I did ask, you didn't believe me, you only ignored or gave me an excuse for why you couldn't help.

I should have put your ass out. We both know damn well you can't live anywhere free of charge. Instead, I bought the excuses and figured out how to pay the bills on my own.

But, time revealed all; you were just spending your money on Danielle, paying her bills and taking her to fancy restaurants. And, of course, you could because you weren't contributing anything to the household. But, you only did what I allowed.

One day, I'm going to laugh when I think back to the time I confused a lesson with a soulmate. You were only a soul tie.

Fuck you for using me to make you happy until you felt you didn't need me anymore and left me wondering where I went wrong. Truth is, I didn't do anything wrong, but stay involved too long with you.

Thank you for leaving me and making me realize my own worth, for helping me discover my own strength that I never knew existed within me. I've learned to love myself more than I love another.

I forgive you for the way you treated me, I forgive you for stabbing me in the back, I forgive you for not seeing my worth. You taught me the lessons I needed to learn. I am stronger because of you. I know what kind of people I need to be around. So, thank you for treating me the way you did because I am better off now. I release all my hate and distaste for you, I am moving on with my life and you no longer have a place in my heart, mind, nowhere. I no longer hold any grudge against you. I forgive you. I just wish you healing, because you're still wounded, and believe it or not, Danielle can't heal you or save you. You have to do your own internal work and confront your own demons.

If I had known everything I know now, I would have just walked away sooner instead of thinking we were going to make it and live happily ever after once we got past the bullshit. I was wrong. Even though you've already moved on and living your life, not thinking of me or the damage you caused, I am finally releasing you back to the universe.

You are nothing more than a tarnished memory and a lesson learned.

"Wow, Jayla, that's deep."

"Yeah, it is! I'm surprised I wrote all that. I was so caught up in the moment, trying to release my feelings that I never bothered to read what I wrote. Reading it now lets me know I'm heading in the right direction in my healing. I'm not that angry anymore, not even bitter; I just want what is better for myself."

I grabbed the lighter from the table and lit a fire under the letter, and watched it form into ashes.

"Sometimes, we have to go down in flames to feel the burn, to know the fire, to be the ash, and then come back to life in the smoke that rises."

- Stacie Martin

CHAPTER 12
Keeping it Real with Self

I've learned a lot of great lessons from a few fucked up people in my life. I'd never again playhouse with a man who is not my husband nor will I allow anyone else to take advantage of me. I would no longer be naive. I couldn't see myself turning a blind eye to the obvious truth when it was standing right in front of me. I was worth so much more than accepting the disrespect and lies for the sake of having someone laying next to me. This experience taught me to refrain from constantly giving someone the benefit of doubt, because in the end, I gave too many benefits, and all I received in return were a broken heart, doubts, and disrespect.

"Jayla, your ex was the problem," Monica said, trying to convince me.

"No, Monica, we weren't dating, according to him; he wasn't an ex-boyfriend, an ex-something. Wait! I know what he was, he was an ex-ample. The perfect example of why I should love myself. It's been a journey, Monica. A lot of this could have prevented, but I have adjusted my crown and it will never come off again.

"Look at you, glowing with self-love. I'm proud of you, J. You have come a long way," Monica said, smiling.

"Thank you, Monica. I truly had to forgive myself for accepting all the things I didn't deserve. I sat with myself and questioned all the reasons why I accepted the lies, cheating, and mental and verbal abuse. The healing process was as ugly as hell. I was afraid to accept the truth. I started by getting to the root of my issues.

"I had to hold myself accountable for my actions, and sometimes, that brought enough guilt and shame.

"See, the truth was, I was ashamed to be the woman that I was; the little girl in me was crying out to be loved, she was hungry for it, desperately wanting to feel wanted, and didn't understand her worth. Unfortunately, that little girl was seeking validation and trying so hard to get it from David. We all eat lies when our hearts are hungry. So, the little girl in me accepted what she felt she deserved, even as a grown woman. Yet, looking back, that was the same little girl who molded me into the woman that I am today.

"My childhood abandonment issues surfaced in my adulthood, and I was in denial. Even when I knew David was full of shit, I kept making excuses for his bad behavior and I held on anyway. I allowed him to take away what I may never get the chance to experience again. I never imagined myself loving a man the way that I loved David. I realized if I had to let go and actually let go sooner, I would be so much farther in my healing. As sincere as my intentions were, had I not tried to fix what was beyond repair and accept the facts, I wouldn't have broken my heart again and again.

"I allowed this man to come into my life and began to get comfortable. I saw all the signs and I ignored the hell out of them because of the love I had for him.

"A part of my healing was accepting that I have toxic traits, too. I held on to people and relationships in my life well past their expiration date because I didn't want to abandon them like my father abandoned me. I knew the pain I felt, And I didn't want to bring myself to doing the very thing that was done to me. But, that wasn't healthy, either. I started therapy because it was time to face my childhood issues, confront my insecurities and dark thoughts, and deeply reason why I felt like I wasn't enough.

"I had to be real with myself and start to do the work. It was uncomfortable, and it still is. But I refuse to repeat this cycle ever again. No matter how uncomfortable the healing process is, I'm committed to it. It's necessary if I ever want to become a better version of myself.

"I am happy, hurting and healing, at the same time; don't ask me how I'm doing it because I don't know, but I'm doing it and I'm so proud of myself. I love the woman I'm becoming. She knows her worth, she has boundaries, and she's motivated and ready to make it all happen for herself. I'm learning everything changes when you begin to love yourself. You no longer send the energy of desperation or need to be filled from the outside. You become a powerful source within yourself that attracts better things. The more you love who you are, the less you seek validation and approval. I don't need anyone else's validation."

"I am so proud of you, Jayla," Monica said, smiling. "When you start taking care of yourself, you start feeling better, you start looking better, and you even start to attract better things. It will always begin and end with you, J. Never feel you aren't enough; we've all been blinded before. Never be embarrassed, to be honest, and open to yourself; it's the first step to healing. Believe me, J, there are women out there that may be experiencing the same situation, or worse. Embrace your pain and turn it into your struggle to triumph. Know that we are here by your side every step of the way."

"Yes!" I said, excitingly. The truthful words blow me away, but I had to admit, she was right. "It will always begin and end with me. Looking back at the girl I used to be and the shit I would allow and tolerate makes me so happy about the woman I am at this very moment. I've come so far."

I began to cry because I remembered my starting point, it was painful, uneasy, and I didn't know my worth. I was a doormat and

● ● ●

allowed someone to treat me poorly just because I loved him and didn't want to lose him. When in reality, I lost myself in the process. I became the woman who kept being mistreated and formed a habit of just brushing it off because I got used to it. I accepted the feeling of not being appreciated and undervalued. I thank God that the old me has died because she has served her purpose. And I vow to myself to never go back to anything or anyone that I had to pray my way out of. A new woman is becoming, and I absolutely love watching her grow daily.

"I'm not afraid of losing anyone anymore, just as long as I never lose myself again. My journey is a beautiful fucking mess, but it's mine. I'm owning it. Hurt people hurt other people, and that's how the pattern gets passed down. I don't want to hurt anyone; so, I'll just stay on this healing journey until I'm completely healed. I'm forgiving everyone who has caused me pain, even if I've never been apologized to. I'm forgiving them because my healing is more important than me holding grudges, which is more suffering. The hurt they caused wasn't about me, it was about the issues within themselves which they haven't dealt with. We all battle our own demons; some people ignore theirs, while others confront them. I'm choosing to confront mine. So, I'll never repeat this again. I refuse to allow myself or anyone to put me back in a situation that I had to pray my way out of. I've run long enough. Never again will anybody have me wondering why I wasn't good enough because I am more than enough. I am beautiful, funny, loyal, and sometimes, a little crazy, but it's out of love. My heart is big, and never again will I allow anyone to take advantage of me. The moment I feel like I have to prove my worth to someone is the moment I walk away.

"I truly loved David, Monica. And now, I just wish him healing. I hope one day, he will confront his own demons and stop running from them."

"It's okay to say you loved him, Jayla, but remember the way he treated you was not love."

"Yes, I know, but I also know I didn't love myself, either. He only did what I allowed him to do, I never taught him how to treat me. And, that was my fault. David may have or have not loved me, but he did change me; he taught and grew me. As fucked up the experience was, I'll never forget it."

"J, girl. I am *so* proud of you. Look at you, sis."

"Thank you. The glow up is so internal. I am focused on myself and only me. I'm moving differently, moving like I love myself, acting like I love myself, and most importantly, I'm keeping it real with myself. I know I deserve to be loved, to be happy, to be treated with respect, and to be appreciated, and nothing less."

"Girl, let me get the champagne glasses, we need to make a toast."

Monica headed to the kitchen to grab our favorite red wine, Poison 1978.

I was so thankful. Monica had been with me every step of my journey. She stood by me through it all and she always tried to enlighten me on my decision making. Sometimes, I listened to her, and other times, I did my own thing. But, in the end, she was always there. And not just Monica, but Denise, Ashton, Keisha, Iesha, Nicole, Teresa, Regina, Myesha, Nikki, Crystal, Kristina, Rose, Erica, Ashley, Joanna, Candice, Vee, and so many others. I was very thankful for my sisterhood of women.

"Let's make a toast, Jayla." Monica handed me a glass, half-filled with red wine. "Here's to self-love and the journey of discovering your whole self. It's terrifying, but it's so liberating. Cheers to growth and gratitude."

"Cheers!"

A wise woman once said "Fuck this shit" and she lived happily ever after.

CHAPTER 13
To the Girl I Was Then

I forgive you, and I love you.

CPSIA information can be obtained
at www.ICGtesting.com
Printed in the USA
FSHW021530240620
71377FS

9 781087 862842